Ewan
Grace

the
BOOKWORM
box

Helping the community, one book at a time

EVAN GRACE

Definition of Realism:

A style of tattooing in which tattoos are depicted as they would be seen in real life. This style focuses more heavily on shading than it does line work. One of the most common styles of realism is portraiture.

MONA

My alarm clock blares, causing me to groan. Those last couple tequila shots last night were such a mistake. Tequila has never been my friend, and I don't know why I thought last night would be any different. I push myself up into a sitting position, but that is a mistake because it feels like my brain is rattling around in my skull. I grab my head as I crawl out of bed and gingerly make my way into the bathroom.

After quickly relieving myself, I grab a bottle of Ibuprofen out of the medicine cabinet. I shake a couple into my hand, pop them into my mouth, and stick my mouth under the faucet. After swallowing them down, I shuffle back to my bed, crawl under the covers, and pray for death.

While buried under my blankets I feel my orange tabby, Peanut, jump on the bed, spin in circles, and then snuggle into my side. As soon as his furry ass begins to purr, I feel my eyes get heavy and let sleep pull me under.

I finally feel semi-human and climb out of bed, heading back into the bathroom. I brush my lavender-colored locks up into a bun on top of my head and jump into the shower. Once I'm scrubbed clean I feel more like myself.

Back in the bedroom, I throw on a pair of black leggings, white camisole, and a blue off-the-shoulder t-shirt. I pad through the house and stick a piece of bread in the toaster and brew some coffee. When the toast is done, I slather it in Nutella and then pour myself a cup of coffee.

Keys jingle, and the front door flies open. My reason for living comes running into the kitchen. "Mommy!"

I catch my daughter and lift her into my arms. "How's my beautiful girl? Were you good for Uncle Miles?"

My brother leans against the open doorway. "She was perfect as always. We had a blast, didn't we, Goober?"

"Yep, Uncle Miles bought me lots and lots of candy."

Of course, he did. My brother has been such an incredible help with Iris, but the man can't ever tell my daughter no. I set her on the ground. "Why don't you go put your dirty clothes in the hamper, and go play with Peanut because I know he missed you."

She kisses me and my brother before running out of the kitchen, yelling for our cat. I grab my brother a cup of coffee, and we sit at the little dinette in front of the window. "How was your girls' night?"

"It was good. Sierra was in rare form and forced

me to do two shots of tequila after mass quantities of beer, and then I had to Uber it home."

There are four daughters and one son in our crazy family. I'm the oldest, then Sierra, Miles is in between us four girls, and then there are Greta and Heidi. We're super close, especially Miles and me. Maybe because he stepped in to be there when Iris' dad split, which was basically the moment the pregnancy test came back positive.

"I'm sure she had to twist your arm too." He stands and pulls me up into a hug. "I'm gonna take off. I've got a book to plot." Miles is a crime fiction writer and, the amazing man he is, a New York Times Bestselling author.

"Have fun with that, and thanks again for keeping Iris." I smile up at him.

"You know I'd do anything for my girls." He calls out goodbye to my daughter, and she comes running out to her uncle.

Iris launches herself into his arms. "Bye, Uncle Miles."

"I'll pick you up tomorrow from Kiddie college."

He leaves, and I smile down at my champagne blonde-haired, blue-eyed angel. "Today is a Mommy/Daughter day. We're going to make a veggie pizza, some chocolate chip cookies, and have couch snuggles."

"Yay! Can you polish my nails?"

I nod. "Of course."

She hops up and down. Her joy is infectious, and we start our Mommy/Daughter day, which indeed ends with snuggles on the couch.

At the end of our day, I tuck her into bed,

brushing her hair out of her face. Iris gives me that smile that's like a balm to my soul. "Sleep well, baby girl."

"I love you," she whispers before rolling to her side and closes her eyes. I don't move right away; I sit and watch as she falls asleep. The steady rise and fall of her chest signals she's out.

From the moment she was born I've watched her sleep more times than I can count. She's the best thing I've ever done, and Iris makes me proud every day.

Is everything always rainbows and unicorns? No, definitely not, but my girl can handle anything thrown our way.

"What do you mean they want to have a meeting about Iris?" I look down at the paper that my brother brought to me after he picked up Iris from Kiddie College. He dropped her off at the tattoo studio I own with my sisters, just like he does every day.

Sierra and I started Sugar and Spice, Ink four years ago. We're all artistic and fell in love with tattoos and piercings. When I decided that I wanted to be a tattoo artist, I met with the one who did a lot of the ink on my body and got him to agree to mentor me. As his apprentice, I cleaned up the shop and answered phones all while learning to tattoo.

Sierra followed in my footsteps almost a year later.

Over the past four years, we've worked our asses

off to make a name for ourselves. Because our studio is exclusively female artists, a lot of people didn't take us seriously. We had to work hard to get word of mouth referrals and prove we were just as talented.

We started getting followers on social media and really used the power of the web to make a name for ourselves. Now, four years later, we've been featured in Ink'd magazine twice, we've been interviewed on Atlanta's morning news, and we were even approached for a reality show, but declined.

I focus back on Miles. "I'm not sure, but they want you there tomorrow morning."

Miles and I step out of my office and head into the main part of the studio. I'm always in awe of the place we've created. The walls are a deep purple, almost an eggplant color, with white swirls. Our tables and chairs are black and chrome.

We have a lot of our artwork on the walls in frames. Some of the tattoos on display are ours, and Greta is on display for her piercings. My favorite photo is of the four of us girls in black Sugar and Spice Ink, sleeveless t-shirts, jean shorts, and red Converse. Heidi did our hair and makeup pin-up girl style.

We find my daughter and Sierra sitting in the waiting area drawing together. Through the entrance to the back, I hear the buzz of a tattoo machine, which is so fucking relaxing.

"Hey, sweet girl, why do they want me to come into the school and talk to them?"

She doesn't look up from her drawing. "I kissed

Max," Iris says it so matter-of-factly that I'm taken aback.

"Who's Max?"

"Max Pena. He's my best friend." She has a smile on her lips. Man, I'm in trouble with this girl.

I sit next to her. "Did he not want you to kiss him, is that why I have to go in?"

She shakes her head. "No, he wanted me to," Iris says.

I don't have much longer to think about that because my last appointment of the day has just shown up. Since I have Iris, my sisters and I agreed it best if I open the shop daily, then I can get out of there by five or six, and I love them for it.

After my appointment, I clean up my workstation and find my girl in my office watching Tangled on my iPad. "Are you ready to head home, baby girl?"

"Yep."

I help her gather her stuff, and then hand in hand we head out to the work area and say our goodbyes.

Once we get home I make us some veggie quesadillas. Iris and I are vegetarians, which I wasn't until I was up in the middle of the night with a newborn and watched a documentary about where our meat comes from. After that, I just couldn't do it. I didn't set out to make Iris one too, but she loves to do what her mom does.

We eat at our little table in the kitchen, and she tells me about her day at Kiddie College. Things have been much easier this summer with Iris able to go there during the day.

After dinner, we snuggle on the couch and watch Modern Family. I can tell she's getting tired when she starts slowly tracing the tattoo of her name on my forearm. Sierra did it for me when Iris was a year old. *Iris* is done in beautiful calligraphy surrounded by gorgeous flowers.

Before she falls asleep, I maneuver her to the bathroom so she can go and then brush her teeth. In her bedroom, she changes into her pink nightgown with sugar skulls all over it.

Iris climbs onto her bed and under her purple butterfly-covered comforter. "Are you all snuggled in?"

"Yes, Mommy." I know my girl's tired. She only calls me Mommy when she's sleepy—much to my chagrin. "Will you lay with me?"

I crawl into bed with her and lean against the headboard. She rests her little blonde head in my lap. "Do you want me to tell you a story?"

She yawns and nods. "Tell me about the day I was born."

Iris has always preferred my stories over the ones in storybooks. I stroke my hand over her soft wavy locks. This is her favorite story, even though it was the easiest labor and delivery ever. "Okay, baby girl. It was two days before your due date, and I was working at a little tattoo studio by Georgia State." My mind goes back to that day…

My back aches, but I ignore it while I continue working on this arm piece. I've worked on this piece for four hours this go around and four hours a month ago. That time was just the outline and details. Today I'm doing the coloring.

I don't know why I keep working. My due date is fast approaching, and it's been so hard to work with my big, protruding belly, but I wanted to keep going as long as possible and to make as much money before his or her arrival.

I never expected to become a mother at twenty-two, especially a single one—no one does—but I'm ready and prepared. I'm just wiping off my client's tattoo. I let her stand and take a look at it in the mirror, smiling as she squeals with delight.

She comes back over, and I wipe some ointment on it before putting plastic wrap over it. I stand to walk her to the counter when I feel a trickle down my leg. "Oh shit."

Buck, the owner, is sitting behind the desk and looks up at my exclamation. The girl I just finished working on turns toward me as well. "Did you just pee your pants?" She laughs.

"No! Of course not, my water just broke." I turn to Buck. "Can you take care of her? I'm calling Sierra."

"You've got it, doll. Good luck."

By the time my sister comes to bring me to the hospital, my contractions are four minutes apart. On the way, I called my mom, and she's meeting us there.

Two hours later, I'm now dressed in only a sports bra and squatting in the water while leaning against the side of the pool, moaning through my contractions. I wanted a natural childbirth, and my midwife had told me about water birth, so that's what I decided I wanted to do.

My mom and Sierra help me through labor as my contractions grow stronger and extremely close together. As my stomach tightens, I rest my head on

16

the side of the pool, moaning softly as my sister fans me, and my mom places a cool washcloth on my neck.

It isn't long before I'm hit with the desire to push. The midwife checks me and says it's time to start pushing. They have me squat in the water, and I begin to push. After pushing for a half hour, they have me reach down to feel the top of my baby's head. I moan as I push with all of my might, and then I feel the baby slip from my body.

They help me grab the baby, and as soon as they lift her out of the water, my beautiful baby starts to cry. The nurse lifts one of the legs and announces, "It's a girl." I begin to cry and hug my daughter to my chest.

Before my mom even cuts the cord, my daughter is latched onto my breast, nursing happily. I'd go through the pain of losing her dad and the pain of her birth to do it all over again.

"What are you going to name her?" Sierra whispers before kissing my cheek.

I've had a couple names picked out for both boys and girls and kept them to myself. I didn't want anyone to influence my decision. I stare at my beautiful baby girl and whisper, "Iris Clementine Collins."

Clementine was my mom's favorite aunt's name, and Iris because I've always loved it for a little girl's name, and it's my favorite flower. Both Aunt and Grandma lean in whispering their "hellos" to my beautiful baby girl.

"Mommy?"

I look down at Iris. "Yes, baby?"

"I love you." It warms my heart every time she tells me that. I can't imagine my life without her in it.

"Love you too." In seconds she's out, hugging her stuffed unicorn to her chest.

I slip out of her bed, turn on her nightlight, and shut the door. Out in the living room, I light my candles, turn out the lights, and grab my meditation pillow. I set everything up in front of the coffee table and ask my *Alexa* to turn on my *Chill Zone* mix.

On my pillow, I get into full lotus position, close my eyes, and clear my mind. I'm not sure how long I've meditated until I open my eyes and see that a half hour has passed. Peanut is sitting in front of me wearing the same bored expression he always does.

"What?"

He tips his head to the side and gives me a "meow". I reach out and scratch behind his ear and then yawn. His fluffy butt follows me as I lock the front door, check on Iris, and he follows me into the bathroom, watching me as I take care of business in here.

I strip down to my tank top and panties, curling up under the sheets and blanket. Peanut jumps on the bed, and I feel him circle his spot behind my knees before he settles in and begins to purr. Not long after, sleep pulls me under.

JOAQUIN

I pull my Range Rover into the parking lot of Edgewood Community College where I've been summoned by Mr. G, the head of the kiddie college that my son Max attends. My son's a good kid, so I'm not sure why Mr. G wants to see me, and my son has said zilch.

I turn to my boy in the backseat. "You ready to go inside, *mijo*?"

My mini-me looks up from his tablet and smiles. "Yeah, Dad." He shuts it off and sets it on the seat. I hop out and meet him at the front. Max may be seven, but he's an old soul. I'm blessed to be his dad.

I'm a single father and have been since he was a toddler. His mother and I were never right for each other. She was the daughter of one of my father's associates. She was a gold-digging whore, and I wasn't going to let her lead me around by my dick.

She trapped me by getting pregnant on purpose,

but she's definitely not mother material. Melina hired a nanny when Max was barely a week old. I, of course, fired the woman because I grew up with nannies, and that wasn't going to be the way my son grew up.

Max only sees her once or maybe twice a year, and it's usually awkward and confuses my boy. His mom's remarried now and someone else's problem—thank God. My cell phone rings as we walk through the halls toward the office of Mr. G. I look and see that it's my secretary, Lauren. "Hold up, Max. I have to take this." I swipe the screen. "Hey, Lauren."

"Sorry to bother you, Mr. Pena." I roll my eyes because I'm constantly telling her to call me Joaquin, but she refuses. "Your three o'clock appointment called and said that they could reschedule for four-thirty. Correct?"

"Yes, as long as they're my last appointment. I promised Max I'd grill burgers tonight, and I don't want to be at the office late." Max smiles up at me, and I ruffle his brown, shaggy hair. I'll need to make him an appointment for a haircut.

"You're all finished after that. I'll make the arrangements. Shall I have coffee waiting?" Lauren is by far the best secretary I've ever had.

"That would be great, thank you." I disconnect and shove my phone inside the pocket of my favorite dove gray Tom Ford two-piece suit. My shirt is a dark salmon pink color, as is the pocket square, and I'm not wearing a tie. On my feet are my favorite Ferragamo Benson burnished leather loafers.

We turn the corner, and I notice a woman with lavender hair braided and hanging over one shoulder. She looks up as we approach, and I'm hit by some unknown force right in the solar plexus. Her eyes are a sparkling cornflower blue. She's got lips made for kissing—*made for kissing?*

Her sun-kissed arms are covered in gorgeous, colorful tattoos. Her white t-shirt hangs off one dainty shoulder, black legging capris cover her legs, and hot pink Converses cover her feet.

"Iris!" Max runs past me to the beautiful little blonde who looks like her mom's twin, but without the lavender hair and ink.

"Max!" She jumps up, and they hug each other. They move to the opposite bench, talking quietly to each other.

"Um … hi. I'm Mona." The lavender-haired beauty holds out her hand. I take her hand, ignoring how soft and small it feels in my much larger one.

"Mr. Pena and Ms. Collins, I'm Mr. G." I turn away from Mona and look at the short man with a major paunch and thinning hairline.

I don't miss the way he looks at Mona, what with the tattoos and the lavender colored hair; she doesn't look like a lot of the parents who bring their kids here. I hold my hand out, squeezing his hand a little harder than necessary. "I'm Joaquin, Max's dad."

"Pleasure," he says and then holds his hand out to Mona. "Please follow me into my office."

We both sit in front of his desk while the kids are led to one of the classrooms to give us some privacy. Mr. G sits behind his desk like he's all high and mighty.

The man looks between the two of us. "Before we begin, will Mrs. Pena be joining us?"

Had the moron read Max's information he'd see that she's not. "His mother is on vacation with her husband. He lives with me full-time."

The idiot nods. "Yesterday, there was a situation with your kids. It was snack time, and the children weren't with the class, so one of the aides went looking for them. She found the two of them by the bathroom, and they were kissing on the mouth." He crosses his arms and looks between us.

Before I can respond, Mona chimes in, "And???"

"Ms. Collins, we don't tolerate that sort of behavior here." The fat prick scowls at her.

Mona leans forward. "I understand that, but did either of them appear to be in distress?"

"Well no, but they're seven years old, and they shouldn't even know about that stuff." Mr. G stares at Mona with a judgmental look on his face.

Out of the corner of my eye, I see Mona tense, gripping the armrests of her chair. She looks ready to snap, and I do the only thing I can think of and put my hand on her knee. I don't miss the way she freezes, and I certainly don't miss the way she trembles under my hand.

I remove it and ignore the fact that it made my dick twitch and my pulse race a little. I open my mouth to speak, but Mona chimes in again. "They shouldn't know about that stuff? I beg your pardon, but people kiss in cartoons. My daughter sees her grandparents kiss. I'm not going to make her feel ashamed that she did it." She stands. "I will talk to her about sneaking off with her friends, and she won't do that again."

"Ms. Collins, I can see you're upset, but the kids aren't in trouble. We just wanted to make you aware of what happened, and maybe you both could discuss with them what is and isn't proper behavior in school." He stands from behind his desk. "I want you to know that your daughter is a joy to have in our creative writing class. She's got a natural gift."

We follow him into the classroom that's off his office and find Iris and Max sitting together coloring. Mona sits across from them. "That's a great tree, Max."

My boy smiles up at her. "Your hair is pretty." He's a charmer, that's for sure.

Mona reaches across the table and grabs Max's arm. "Thank you. Iris, come give me a hug goodbye. Uncle Miles will pick you up and bring you to the studio, okay."

"Yes, Mom. I love you."

I walk around the table, ruffling Max's hair. "I'll be back after my meeting to get you. I love you, *mijo*."

As soon as I leave the classroom I spot Mona up ahead, but I don't rush to catch up with her; there's no point. Like I said, she's not my type. Plus, my focus needs to be on my son, not pussy.

I head downtown to my office. I have to prep before my meeting. My partners and I keep things flexible, which is great and I'm able to get off at a reasonable time so I can still be a father to my boy. My father is a workaholic, and growing up I watched as my mom grew to resent him.

They both began screwing around on each other, and that led to a nasty divorce. Now they live on opposite sides of the country. Dad is on marriage number four, and Mom is on marriage number two, but things are rocky.

When I divorced Max's mom I swore, I was never going to get married again. She reminded me exactly why I wanted to always stay single, but I'll never regret my boy. Once I reach the office, I park in the garage and head to the elevator, taking it up to my floor.

I share a floor with a marketing agency, but they're on one side, and I'm on the other. My partners and I have had our own brokerage firm for the past three years. Before that, I worked for my father's firm. When he decided to retire down in Florida, his partners became mine, and his clients followed me.

Our receptionist for the office greets me from his desk. "Good morning, Shane."

"Morning. I love that suit; it's my favorite," he says with his usual flourish. The man basically runs the office and is my personal shopper. He and Lauren are the backbone of the company. I'd be lost without either of them. He flirts with me a little, but it doesn't bother me; he's harmless.

I shake my head and head toward the back. Lauren stands as I approach. "How was the meeting?"

"My son and a little girl snuck off, and when they found them they were kissing on the lips. Iris is his best friend I guess. Anyway, the guy was a pompous ass. Iris' mom let him have it."

24

"My boys were rascals like that when they were his age. I'm sure it was harmless." Her boys are in their early twenties, and even though I'm thirty she treats me like one of her kids, but not in an obnoxious way. "I've got the conference room set up for your meeting. When they arrive, shall I bring you coffee?" She follows me into my office.

"That would be great." Lauren hands me my messages and then closes the door behind her, letting me get to work.

I pull into the winding driveway that leads to the modern cottage I bought two years ago in the Buckhead district when I decided Max and our damn dog, Fluffy, needed more room to play.

When we moved here, my cousin Victoria moved in with us. Her mom is my dad's sister, and she's about as maternal as my dad is paternal. Thank God we have each other. She's been a big help with my son.

Her moving in with me was only supposed to be temporary, but with as much as she does for us, we decided we'd keep our arrangement until she either needed to move on or I met someone.

Victoria was given the task of decorating. I only had two stipulations: nothing girly and nothing bachelor pad-ish. Don't get me wrong, I have expensive taste, but I wanted a home that my son could feel like he could play in.

I grew up in a home where I was told not to make a mess and to never run around and be a kid. I pull into the garage and hop out with my boy following me. As soon as we step inside, the scent of tomatoes hits me. Victoria is a maestro in the kitchen.

"*Tia* Victoria, we're home." Max runs through the mudroom and into the kitchen where I find him hugging my cousin.

"How was school? What did they want to talk to you about?" She asks me the second part.

"Max and a girl named Iris were caught kissing," I say.

"Oh, I love Iris. Why did you kiss her?" She squats in front of Max.

The little shit rolls his eyes. "She's my best friend." The way he says it he should've ended with a *duh*. Max crosses his arms. "They wouldn't let us sit together."

I'm not a hundred percent sure how to handle this because I don't want him to feel shame. "If she's your best friend, why did you kiss her?"

"You kiss *Tia* Victoria, and she's your best friend." Well, he has me there.

"That's true, buddy, she is, and yes, I kiss her, but only on the cheek or forehead—not the lips, definitely not the lips. Got it?"

He nods. "I've got it. Do you think she could come over and play sometime?"

Iris' mom, with her lavender hair, pops into my head. They're both beautiful, and I imagine Mona's natural hair is the same as her daughter's. She definitely had some gumption, not letting that fat fuck shame her. I push thoughts of her away—not going there.

26

"Yeah, maybe we could have her over one afternoon." I walk over and look at what Victoria has cooking. "I was going to grill burgers."

"Go ahead, this sauce is for dinner tomorrow night. I just wanted to get it done so we didn't have to worry about it tomorrow. I've got the patties already made and in the fridge." She looks down at my son. "You can help me make homemade fries."

I head to the master bedroom, which is on the first floor, and change into a pair of jeans and a t-shirt. Fluffy comes tearing into my room; he must've been outside when we got home. He reads me his puppy riot act for being gone. I pick his white curly-haired ass up and hug him to my chest while he licks my neck.

He's a Shih Tzu/Poodle mix and is the best dog we could ask for. "Are you a good boy?" Fluffy pants in my face. "Your breath is horrid." I scratch behind his ear and then set him down.

He follows me to the two people I love more than anything.

MONA

I pace the office at the back of our tattoo studio. My stomach is in knots, and I thought I was ready, but I'm not. I shake out my hands that haven't stopped tingling since earlier today.

It started like any other day. Iris went with me to run errands for the studio, and then we stopped for an ice cream cone before we went to the grocery store. We'd just sat down to eat our cones when Iris' dad, my ex, Sam, walked in with the woman he was with the last time I ever saw him.

He was holding the hand of a little boy who looked just like him. The woman had a very pregnant belly. Why did it hurt so much to see that … oh right, that's because he threw me and our daughter away so easily.

"Honey, let's take our cones and go." I stood and held out my hand to her.

"I thought we couldn't eat in the car."

Iris was right. I've never let her eat in the car.

"Today's a special day, and you get to, but please be careful."

"I will, Mommy, but why is today special?"

I didn't know what to tell her, and I hate lying to her. It was only to protect her from the pain that I suffered through when he left us. "It just is, baby girl."

We made it up and out before getting noticed, or so I thought. "Mona?" Fuck me, I tried to force my feet to carry us out the door, but I was frozen. He reached us, and I tucked Iris partially behind me. "How are you?"

How am I? That's what he wanted to know? "I'm good, Sam. Well, it was good seeing you." We hustled outside, but the world was looking to knock me down a peg.

"Mona, wait up." I turned and watched him hustle toward me. I couldn't believe I'd ever found him attractive. Oh sure, in a sense he was good looking, but knowing what a piece of crap he was, I now found him ugly. "I'm glad I ran into you. Can we meet for lunch sometime this coming week?"

My heart started beating a rapid staccato in my chest. "Why?"

He glanced at Iris and then back at me. "I just want to talk about some stuff."

"I don't know if that's a good idea. You made things pretty clear eight years ago."

"I want to make things right. I was young and stupid back then."

I shook my head in disbelief. "You were thirty." He was eight years older than me. My entire family hated him and then hated him more when he split after getting me pregnant.

The man was persistent, and if I didn't meet with him he'd badger me until I did. I sighed, "Fine, why don't you stop by the studio around seven. We can talk then."

He smiled, and it made me uneasy. "Great, I'll be there."

Now I keep watching the time and waiting for Sam to show up and drop whatever bomb he's going to. I have a feeling he's going to want to see her. I don't want to share my daughter with him. He doesn't deserve to know how special she is. He left without looking back and damaged my heart irrevocably.

I grab my bag and fish out a mint, popping it into my mouth, and use some powder on my face. I told my sisters that he was coming—only so they would be prepared. I've had to beg them to not approach when he comes.

Because I do know that he's coming to talk about Iris.

When the chime above the door goes off, signaling that someone's opened the front door, I rush down the hall and find him standing in the entryway, looking around. He spots me and smiles. "Your studio is incredible."

"Thank you. We worked really hard on making this place what it is. Let's go talk in the office." The quicker we do this, the quicker I can get him out of here.

He grabs the chair and sits in front of the desk. I sit in the chair next to him and turn it so we're facing each other. "What did you need, Sam?"

Again, my pulse races because I don't know what he's about to say. He leans forward. "I wanted to apologize about the way I left, and that I didn't step up when you told me you were pregnant."

"It was a long time ago, and we've been just fine." Honestly, we have been.

Sam nods. "It's clear you have. I know I don't have a right to ask, but I'd like to get to know her. I'll do whatever you want, however you want it."

Blood rushes in my ears, and I want to scream; instead, I bring up the one and only time he saw her. "The last time you saw her you didn't even look at her. She ran right past your table with me following behind. I know you saw me because you looked right at me, or I'm sorry—you looked right through me."

"What do you want me to say, Mona? I'm a dick, I know it. I don't know. I've got kids now, and I've been thinking about her a lot lately. I told my wife about her, and she's honestly pissed at me for not being involved."

He scrubs his hand over his face. "I know I don't have the right to ask for visitation, and I know you're not going to say yes right away, but I'd love for you to think about it. I'm also going to pay you back child support until I'm caught up."

"I don't need your money. I haven't asked for anything since you walked away," I state calmly.

"I know you haven't, but I want you to take it regardless. Open a savings account for, um … her."

For fuck's sake, he doesn't even remember her name. I sent him one message when she was born and told him her name. "Her name is Iris."

"Iris?" He scrunches his nose like he used to when he thought I was being uncouth. "What's her middle name?"

"Her full name is Iris Clementine Collins."

My hackles rise when he starts to laugh. He shakes his head at me. "Iris Clementine? Jesus Christ," he mutters.

I stand. He almost had me fooled. "I think we're done." I march toward the door and throw it open. "Bye, Sam."

He stands, stopping in front of me. "I don't understand why you couldn't just give her a normal name."

"Irises are my favorite flower, and Clementine was my mom's favorite aunt's name. It's got character just like she does. If you can't accept her then you don't need to get to know her."

Ugh, he rolls his eyes at me, making me want to slap his stupid face. "You're looking good." He leans back, looking me up and down.

"A tiger never changes his stripes," I mutter.

"Whatever, I just want to get to know my kid."

I shake my head. "Your kid? If, and when, it happens, it'll be on *my* daughter's terms." Emphasis on *my*.

"I'll stop by in a week to talk again. Later." He walks by me and disappears down the hall. God, that went south quickly, but I'm glad his true colors came out. My guess is I'll never see him, or any child support. Whatever, we've been doing fine without him.

Greta comes stomping down the hall. "The dickhead is gone." She crosses her arms over her chest.

I nod. "Thank goodness."

"What did he want?"

I shrug. "He wants to know his daughter and to start paying child support." I lean forward. "He couldn't remember her name, and then he laughed when I told him what it was. Do you believe that shit?" I tip my head back. "I swear he looked me up and down like he was hitting on me. He's got a wife who has given him one kid and one on the way. I feel dirty now." I fake shiver.

"I ought to go kick his ass for making fun of my niece's name … fucking prick."

I hook my arm through hers, and we head back into the parlor. My sisters look at me and once they see me smile, they relax. No one can get the Collins girls down.

I ask Greta to fill Sierra and Heidi in on Sam's visit. I need to pick up my daughter from my brother's place. When I pull up in front, it's already a little past eight. Glenn, his doorman, holds the door open as I walk toward him. "Good evening, Ms. Collins."

"Good evening, Glenn."

I walk through the door. "Your daughter is quite the young lady. You should be very proud."

"Thank you, I am." In the elevator I hit penthouse one and ride it up to his floor. When I step off, I use the key my brother gave me and let myself in. I find my brother sitting on his plush brown leather sofa with the TV on mute, typing away on his laptop. "Hey, brother."

He turns and smiles. "Hey, sister."

"How was she tonight?"

Miles sets his laptop down and stands, hugging me. "She was perfect as always. We decided to work on our own book tonight. Iris titled it, My Favorite Uncle." I roll my eyes, and he shrugs. "What? I can't help it that I am."

"You're her only uncle. Is she in your room laying down?"

He leads me down the hall, and I find my girl curled up in the middle of his bed, fast asleep with her hands curled under her chin.

"Sometimes I can't believe she's mine," I whisper.

Miles wraps his arm around my shoulders. "Greta called me before you got here and told me about Sam's visit.

I sigh and lean my head against his chest. "For a brief second I thought he might truly want a relationship with her. First, he forgot her name, and then laughed when I told him what it was. He even had the nerve to check me out. I'm sure if I wait it out then he'll eventually disappear again."

"How did this even come about? I thought you haven't seen him."

"I haven't, but when Iris and I stopped for ice cream, he and his little family came in. We tried to sneak out, but he saw me and followed us out. It doesn't matter."

I grab Iris' bag as Miles scoops her up in his arms, helping me get her downstairs and loaded in my car. He opens my door for me, but first I hug him. "Thanks for keeping her."

"Always, Mo." Miles stands on the sidewalk

watching us until we pull away.

Once we're home, I attempt to carry my girl in the house, but I definitely struggle. I don't bother changing her out of her clothes; I just cover her up. Peanut comes in and rubs against my ankle, giving me a little *meow.*

"Hey, handsome." I scratch behind his ear before he jumps up onto Iris' bed, curling up with her. On my way out of her room, I turn her nightlight on. It covers the inside of her room with little unicorns.

In the kitchen I turn on my warmer, and in no time the scent of lavender fills my room. I'm tense from the situation earlier and decide to do some yoga. I suck at it and spend more time falling over. At least it takes my mind off Sam.

After yoga and a glass of wine, I lock up the house. Before heading to bed, I peek in on Iris and see that she's asleep and Peanut is curled up against her chest. I leave them and head into my bathroom and get ready for bed.

JOAQUIN

"Dad, guess what?" Max comes racing out the doors of the school with an envelope in his hand. He waves it wildly in my face before letting me take it from him. "Look, look!"

I open it and see that it's an end of summer party, hosted by Mona and Iris Collins at Sugar and Spice, Ink. A party at a tattoo studio? Yes, I looked her up. The lavender-haired woman has been creeping into my thoughts, on and off over the past couple of weeks since we met. Her tattoo career is definitely impressive.

She and her sisters have one of the highest rated tattoo studios in the area. The pictures I've seen of her are stunning. Her hair color has been baby blue, platinum, and lavender, of course. She's got that pinup girl look in a lot of the photos, and damn if they weren't sexy. My favorite one that she's topless, but her hands cover her breasts and she's giving an exaggerated wink.

The ink that covers a lot of her is beautiful. Whoever did them did a phenomenal job. I won't lie, I've never been a fan of tattoos on women, but lately I've been liking them more and more. The other night I jerked off thinking about her, which was a first, but the fantasy in my head was so vivid.

"Dad?"

I shake my head. "Sorry, bud. What?"

"Can I go? Please?" He bounces up and down in front of me.

How can I tell him no? I can't, of course. "Sure, of course." That might give me a chance to get to know Miss Mona Collins a bit more.

"Can I RSVP?" Max asks.

I hand him my phone and the invitation, and he presses each number slowly and carefully. He concentrates so hard his tongue peeks out the corner of his mouth. Max holds the phone to his ear, and I hear the feminine voice that answers. "Hello?"

"This is Max Pena, and me and Iris are best friends, so I'll be at her party." He says it all in one breath.

I can hear Mona respond. "That's great, Max. I'll let Iris know you'll be there. You take care of yourself, okay?"

"I will—I promise. Tell Iris I miss her already." This kid is laying it on thick.

Her melodic laugh can be heard through the line. "I'll be sure to tell her as soon as I get home. I'm sure she misses you too."

"Of course she does." His voice is like, duh. "Bye, Iris' mom."

"Goodbye, Maximum." My son hands me my

phone, and I quickly program Mona's number into it. I convince myself it's just for Max and no other reason.

Once that's done, Max climbs into the backseat, settling on his booster seat.

We get home, and we're on our own for dinner. Victoria is working and then going out after. I can hold my own in the kitchen as long as it's a pretty simple recipe. "Bud, go get Fluffy and take him out while I start dinner."

While he lets the dog out, I scan the refrigerator looking for something to cook, but I'm not finding anything that looks good. My cousin has spoiled me with her superior cooking. I hear the back door open, and seconds later my son and Fluffy are running circles around the kitchen island.

"Hey, dude, do you want to go out for pizza?"

Max jumps and throws his fists in the air. "Yes! Can we go to Gino's?"

It's a little family pizzeria that has the best thin crust around. We found it by mistake one day, and it just became our spot. "Yeah, we can go to Gino's. I'm going to change; make sure Fluffy has water and food, then go wash your hands." I head to my bedroom to change into a pair of jeans, a t-shirt, and my beat-up black Chucks.

Max impatiently waits by the door to the garage. I grab my keys, wallet, and phone. We make our way toward the restaurant. I park on the street a few buildings away.

The scent of tomato sauce hits me when we step inside. Jacque, Gino's wife, comes over to us with a smile on her face. "Hello, Pena men. How are you?"

She squeezes my shoulder before hugging Max.

We follow her to a table. "We're good, thanks." She sits us in front of the window. I look to Max. "What kind of pizza should we get?"

Max taps his chin, pretending to ponder it. "Sausage?"

"Okay, sausage it is." We order our drinks and breadsticks to start.

I've always promised myself that I wouldn't be one of those parents who spends the whole meal staring at my phone, but sometimes work causes me to be on it more than I'd like.

Max colors on his placemat. "Are you excited about school starting back up? You're going to be in second grade."

He doesn't look up when he answers. "I am, but I'm sad Iris won't be there. She goes to a different school." I wonder if I should be worried about his attachment to the little girl.

"Max!" Speaking of the little blonde, she runs right up to our table, and I spot Mona weaving through the tables toward us.

My son jumps up and wraps his arms around Iris. I stand, looking at Mona. "Hello, Miss Collins."

"Mr. Pena." She smiles up at me before turning toward the kids. "Hi, Maximum." Her smile is luminous, *luminous?* That's the second time she's called my son that, and by the look on my boy's face—he loves it.

"Hi, Iris' mom."

"Call me Mona, okay?" she tells Max, while unconsciously playing with her daughter's ponytail.

"Do you want to join us?"

She smiles up at me, and my fingers itch to reach out and touch her skin. "Are you sure? We don't want to intrude."

"Not at all."

We end up sitting side by side because the kids wanted to sit next to each other. I watch Mona out of the corner of my eye while she munches on a breadstick. I know I need to stop before she catches me, but I just can't force myself to look away.

The kids have been chatting quietly while they color. I definitely need to make sure they're able to see each other.

"What made you decide to become a tattoo artist?"

She takes a sip of her water and turns to me. "I've always been artistic; I paint, sketch, and have worked with charcoals. When I turned nineteen and was away at school, I got my first tattoo." Mona turns her bicep, showing me a small tattooed Belle from Beauty and the Beast. "I became obsessed. I ended up doing an apprenticeship at that same studio. The moment I held that tattoo machine in my hand I felt complete. Two of my sisters followed my path, but my sister Greta—she's our piercer."

"That's amazing that you found your passion so young."

"Yeah, my parents weren't thrilled at first, but they saw how serious I took it. It also helped that they saw the skill level I had. After that, they became my biggest cheerleaders. I still paint sometimes, but I don't have a lot of free time. What is it that you do?" We're interrupted by Jacque bringing our pizzas. She smiles at the four of us and

41

then walks away.

"You don't eat meat?" I look down at their veggie pizza.

"Not since Iris was a newborn. I watched a documentary one night when I was up late feeding her, and it was about meat processing plants. I couldn't do it after that."

We fix plates for the kids, and they begin to dig in. "Back to your question earlier, I'm an investment broker. I'm a partner in a brokerage firm."

"Is that something you've always wanted to do?"

"No, but I've always been into the stock market. Right out of college I worked at my father's firm and learned a lot. When my dad decided to retire and relocate, his clients and partners stayed with us." I take a bite of my pizza and close my eyes savoring the flavorful sauce.

We're all silent when we first start eating. I smile because both kids have sauce on their faces, but they're definitely enjoying themselves. Conversation begins between us and flows like we've known each other forever. She tells me about her sisters and brother and the close relationship they all have.

Jacque interrupts us when bringing the checks. I grab both of them, and when Mona reaches for hers, I tell her that I've got it.

"Joaquin, I can't let you do that."

"Yes, you can. It was good for the kids to see each other. Max is missing Iris already." I don't get the look that crosses her face, and she turns to wipe Iris' face off. She pulls out another wipe and starts

42

working on Max. "Thank you."

"Sure, it's the least I could do. Thank you for dinner." She gets down in front of Max. "It was good seeing you, sir. We'll see you at our party."

"Okay, see you later," he says, giving her a big, bright smile and a hug.

Mona stands, shaking her head. "Thank you again. Iris, thank Max's dad for dinner."

"Thank you for the pizza." She smiles up at me, and I swear my heart flutters. Iris then hugs my son and tells him bye."

Hand in hand they walk toward the door, and I won't lie that my eyes follow her ass the whole way. Max pulls on my hand, bringing me out of my Mona fog. We stop at the counter so I can pay.

Jacque takes both tickets. "Was that your girlfriend?" She smiles at us.

I shake my head. "God no," I say it a little too loud.

She looks at me and then past me … her face pales.

I turn slowly and find Mona standing there. "I, uh, forgot my phone. Um … I thought I'd also leave the tip." She hustles past us with Iris running to catch up.

"I'm so sorry, Joaquin," Jacque says as she hands me my receipt.

"It's not your fault, Jacque. This is all on me."

Max doesn't know what's going on, thankfully, and takes my hand as we head to my SUV to head home.

Once Max is showered and tucked into bed, I head into my room. I toss my watch and wallet on top of my dresser before stripping down into my boxer briefs and climb into bed. I grab my phone off my nightstand and am thankful I saved Mona's number when we called to RSVP to the party.

I open the texting app and type her a quick message.

Joaquin: Hey, it's Joaquin. I'm sorry about earlier. I just wanted Jacque to back off. She meddles.

I wait for the black dots to start dancing, and when they finally do, I sigh with relief. I know I'm a dick sometimes, and honestly, I don't mean to be.

Mona: It's okay. I seriously get it.

Joaquin : Get what?

The dots start bouncing again.

Mona: Look at me, and look at you. It's very clear that we're not together. Our kids just happen to be best friends.

I take a minute to think of my response.

Joaquin : You know, we could become friends too.

It's a good five minutes before the dots begin again.

Mona: Sure, why not.

That's the last message I get from her. We'll see how a friendship goes considering our children are the only things we have in common.

JOAQUIN

I step inside Ray's in the City and look around, trying to spot my buddy Nick. I head to the hostess stand that's empty, but in no time a buxom blonde saunters over to me with an exaggerated sway of her hips. "Hello. Welcome to Ray's. A table for one?"

I smile because she is fucking hot and exactly the kind of woman I'd hook up with, but a lavender-haired, tattooed beauty keeps popping into my mind. She's been on my mind since the night we had pizza, but we haven't spoken.

I know it's shitty especially after telling her I want to be her friend, but I've needed these past few days to get my shit together. I won't lie that I want her, physically, but that would be such a bad idea. Not when our kids clearly care about each other a lot.

"I'm meeting someone. I'll take a table in the bar if you've got one."

"Absolutely, follow me." She leads me to a table. "Here you go. Let me know if you need *anything*."

The hostess licks her lips in clear invitation.

The waiter comes, dragging my attention to him, and I give him my drink order. By the time he returns with my beer, Nick comes walking in. "Joaquin !" The man is loud and sometimes has no filter, but he's my best friend and has been since we were in high school.

I stand, and the man who makes *me* look small grabs me in a bear hug, practically lifting me off the floor. "Looking good, brother." Nick sets me down. "Did you get a load of the tits on the hostess?"

The table across from us gives Nick a dirty look, but the man is oblivious. We sit, and the waiter takes his drink order, and we order appetizers.

"How's my boy doing?"

Just the mention of my son and I can't help but smile. That kid can take me from a bad mood to a good one in seconds. "He's great. He's had a blast at the kiddie college you suggested."

"Good, I'm glad. How's business? You happy?"

"Nick, I'm happy. I've got steady clientele. I'm making a helluva living, and my boy isn't suffering because of it." I take a drink of my beer. "I was thinking about going to the lake the weekend after next if you're interested."

We love going down to Lake Oconee, which is only about an hour and a half away. Max and I usually spend the whole weekend there. I either book us one of the cottages or a suite.

"Yeah, that might be fun. The single moms are always hot and ready to fuck."

I can only shake my head because everyone is looking at him. Our appetizer arrives, and I'm thankful for the brief reprieve because Nick's silent while we eat.

I'm popping my last bite of calamari into my mouth when feminine laughter draws my attention to the opening to the bar.

A platinum blonde with full tattoo sleeves comes walking in, followed by a blonde with hot pink tips, and bringing up the rear is a brunette with multiple piercings, her arm looped through the lavender-haired beauty who has unknowingly implanted herself in my brain.

She looks like a naughty librarian. Her hair is up in a bun, she's wearing black-rimmed glasses, and the white t-shirt has a multi-colored skull on it. The black pencil skirt highlights her curves.

I turn my attention back to Nick. "Business good?" He's a restaurateur.

"I'm thinking about purchasing another restaurant. I've also got some news." He leans forward. "The owner of the Atlanta Fire contacted me." It's our stadium football team. "He wants me to be his partner and co-own the team. Motherfucker must be hurting for cash. I do it, you know what that means: luxury suite, free food, booze and cheerleaders.

"That's a pretty sweet deal. If you want, I'm sure my father would look over the contract."

Nick nods. "Great, I'm going to use the restroom. I'll be right back." Nick gets up and walks by Mona's table. I shake my head because he stops—I don't know what he says to them, but they all start laughing. He backs away from them with his hands up.

The platinum gives him a little wave and blows him a kiss. I'm sure Nick will be slipping her his number or asking for hers before we leave.

My eyes go to Mona; she gives me a smile and a small wave. I give her a chin lift, and then the waiter stops at the end of my table setting mine and Nick's food down. I'm thankful for the distraction—no need to lead her on.

Nick comes back and leans in. "Do you see the table over there? My God, they're hot, and they're sisters."

I glance at them and take a closer look at the ones I can see, which is Mona and the one with hot pink tips, and there's definitely a strong resemblance. I turn away before they catch me gawking.

After lunch, we pay our bills then head toward the door, but against my better judgment, I stop right next to Mona. She looks up at me nervously, and I can't help but smile. I lean down and speak softly in her ear. "Good to see you, Miss Collins. I look forward to seeing you at the party."

Her cheeks turn a delicious shade of pink. "You too, Mr. Pena."

I turn away, and as I get further from the table I hear one of her sisters say quite loudly, "Oh my God, who the fuck was that?"

I smile as I walk out of the bar. Against my better judgment, I'm looking forward to seeing her again.

MONA

I watch the clock, and my stomach turns. Only two kids have shown up, and I'd invited over thirty. I knew there was a possibility of this happening; I was hoping that in this day and age that people would be over their preconceived notions about people with tattoos.

My daughter was so excited about the party that she was up at five am and begged me to do her hair. After breakfast, that is what I did. Her champagne-colored locks are in twists and braids and then up in a ponytail.

She decided to wear little black biker shorts with a purple tutu, and up top she's wearing layered tank tops. Iris insisted that I dress like her, but instead of twists and braids my hair is up in a bun on top of my head. My tutu is lavender, and I'm wearing a fitted t-shirt instead of a tank top. We're wearing matching black Converse. When we got to the studio my sisters were already decorating, and I laughed because my daughter must've called them all and told them what to wear because we're all dressed alike.

I know my daughter's trying to be a good hostess, but I don't miss the way she keeps watching the door, waiting for Max to show up. The past week they've been FaceTiming each other at night—even going as far as to FaceTiming while we shopped for school supplies.

Joaquin and I have talked some, but most of the time just about the kids. We hope that once they start school their friendship lasts and doesn't fizzle out.

The parents of the kids who are here already haven't really spoken to me or my sisters, but I'm used to it, and they've been looking down their noses at us since they got here.

The party theme is unicorns and tutus, so all of the kids are wearing headbands with a sparkly horn coming out of their foreheads. My sisters and I are all wearing them too. I know we look ridiculous, but I don't care because I'd do anything for my girl.

I glance outside and see a fancy Range Rover pull into the parking lot. Iris vibrates with excitement as she runs toward the front door. My belly does a stupid little dip I force myself to ignore as I spot Joaquin in all his dark and handsome glory. The man is sex on a stick when he's in a suit, but when he's in jeans and a t-shirt like now, he's dangerously hot.

His eyes are covered in aviators, and his dark brown hair is perfectly styled, like usual. Joaquin opens the back door, and Max hops out. God, that little boy is so precious. How can a mother not want to raise her son?

I laugh when I realize Joaquin and his boy are wearing semi-matching shirts. Max's says Padawan, and his dad's says Jedi Master. I honestly never thought that Joaquin could have a sense of humor. He reminds me too much of Sam: rich, uptight, and arrogant.

Iris tears out of the building and runs to Max. I smile as the two embrace like they haven't seen each other in forever. Joaquin leads the kids inside, and Iris drags the boy who is the exact replica of his dad over to me.

"Look who's here?" Her voice is a borderline shriek.

"Hey, Maximum. I'm glad you could make it. Iris, why don't you kids have your aunts paint your faces." All five kids take off running into the back. I sigh and then say quietly, "No one else RSVP'd. It was probably a mistake to have it here. I mean, it's not unsafe. We keep the needles, ink, and machines locked up. Thank you for bringing him." I look up into Joaquin's dark chocolate eyes, and my belly does that little dip again.

"You're welcome, and no, I don't think it was a mistake to have it here." He looks around. "Do you need anything?"

"No, but thank you for asking. Help yourself to snacks and water or soda."

The party goes well, and Iris doesn't seem too concerned that only three other kids showed up. Hell, I think if it had just been Max she wouldn't have cared. Oh, she's happy the other kids came, but Max is her best friend.

I check on the kids and see they're all in chairs waiting. Iris is already done and chatters happily to the other kids. The other parents smile as they watch their children's faces get painted.

As soon as Joaquin steps in the back, the two moms here with their daughters sigh; I swear. They both stand a little taller, thrusting their boobs out and being very obvious about it.

Once face painting is done, I take pictures of the kids, and they head outside to draw with chalk on the sidewalk in front of the studio with Greta. Joaquin is walking around the room looking at the pictures of our work. My sisters come over and introduce themselves to him. I roll my eyes because they're practically drooling on him.

"Sierra, why don't you grab the sandwiches and chips so everyone can eat." My sister looks at me and winks before heading to the office to grab the food.

"Joaquin, do you want to bring the kids in, in about five minutes?" He nods and heads outside.

Heidi pounces as soon as he leaves. "Girl, he is F. I. N. E. If you don't want him, can I have him?"

"I don't know what you're talking about." I try to walk away from her, but she stops me with a hand on my arm.

"He's totally into you."

I shake my head. "Our kids are best friends, that is it. Don't read too much into it. Plus I can guarantee that I'm not his type."

As I walk out front, I hear her shout, "You're blind, sister dear." I ignore her comment and help get the food set up, but my super-efficient sister already has everything ready.

I walk toward the door and look out the window to see that Iris is animatedly talking to Joaquin, who is smiling down at her. I used to long for her father to smile at her like that, but I'm not sure that's ever going to happen.

An arm wraps around my waist, and I smile at Sierra as she hugs me. "It looks like you're not the only one smitten." She's not wrong about that, even though he's got heartbreak written all over him.

I open the door and call out, "Time to eat." The kids follow by Joaquin, Greta, and the two moms come inside. Iris and I got veggie sandwiches, and we got turkey for everyone else. We also have pasta salad, veggies and dip, potato chips, and cake for dessert, of course.

After everyone finishes, the kids are playing games with my sisters. The moms are flirting shamelessly with Joaquin, so I busy myself with clean-up duty.

"Mona?" I turn to Christopher's dad, the other little boy who came. "We haven't officially met, but I'm Brad."

I hold out my hand. "Nice meeting you. You have a very sweet and polite boy. I hope he's having a good time."

"Thank you for saying that. He had a hard time after his mom and I split. Honestly, he wasn't sure if he wanted to come or not, but I thought it would be good for him. Now, I see I made the right decision." The way he says it makes my skin crawl. His eyes do a lazy perusal of my body, and I slowly inch away.

"Maybe we could take the kids and do something sometime."

"That's a really nice offer, but..."

Before I can finish my thought, an arm wraps around my shoulders. I look up to find Joaquin staring at Brad. "Hey, baby, did you need some help cleaning up?" He smiles at me and then looks at the other man. "I'm Joaquin, and you are?"

"I'm Brad; are you two together?" He looks between the two of us.

"Yes, Brad, we are. I'm a lucky guy."

Brad nods then moves over to my sisters. I can only shake my head.

I lean into Joaquin. "Thank you for that. He was starting to creep me out," I say quietly.

He lets go of me, and I already miss his warmth, which is definitely not a good sign, but I push that feeling away for the time being.

The party ends a short while later, and the only people left are my sisters, Joaquin, and Max. I'm surprised when Joaquin starts the task of cleaning up. I hand Iris my iPad and have her and Max go watch a movie on it in the office so they're out of the way.

After we finish up, Joaquin runs the garbage out to the dumpster. Greta comes over and bumps me with her hip. "I really like him. He was so sweet to Iris when we were outside earlier."

She doesn't get a chance to tell me why because Joaquin walks back in.

I lead him down the hall to the office, and we step inside finding both kids asleep on the little loveseat we have in there. "Aren't you worried the face paint is going to get on the upholstery?"

"No, Iris has spent a lot of time here over the years. I've become a pro at shampooing furniture."

I turn to look at him, and he's staring down at me with a strange look on his face. "Are you okay?" I whisper softly.

Joaquin whispers back, "Tu erres otra cosa." *You are something else*. His face lowers, and his breath hits my lips. I lean in, meeting him halfway.

Our lips brush softly, and my knees quake. If

they're doing this now from just a chaste kiss, I can only imagine what'll happen if he *really* kisses me.

"Ahem… Sorry to interrupt. I thought I'd see how the party was."

Joaquin pulls away from me, and I look around him and find my brother smirking at us. "This is Joaquin, Max's dad." I point to Miles. "This is my brother, Miles Collins."

My brother sticks his hand out, and they shake hands. "Wait, you write that crime series, right?"

Miles nods. "Yeah. Have you read the latest?"

"No, I'm two books behind. You write amazing stories." I'm kind of finding this entertaining. Joaquin is totally fangirling over my baby brother.

"Thank you. I appreciate that."

They make small talk for a few minutes before Joaquin picks up Max, tells us goodbye, and disappears out of the office.

"I didn't mean to interrupt," Miles says before he sits next to sleeping Iris.

I shake my head. "You didn't interrupt anything ... unfortunately."

"How was the party?"

"It went well. Only four kids showed up, but I think they had a good time. As you can see, your niece is wiped." I reach down, stroking her hair.

Iris rolls over and lets out a little fart, causing Miles and me to laugh hysterically.

"We've got everything picked up and shut down. Are you okay if we leave?" Sierra comes into the room, wrapping her arms around Miles. "This guy can protect you."

"Of course. Thank you for helping so much with

the party, and thanks for cleaning up."

Sierra comes to me, and I stand, wrapping my arms around her. "You know I'd do anything for our girl."

Heidi and Greta come in as well, and I thank them for helping with the party. When it's just Miles, Iris, and me, he begins grilling me. "Tell me about Joaquin?"

"There's nothing to tell. I mean, sure he's hot, and our sort of kiss was off the charts, but he reminds me too much of Sam." I fake shiver.

"What do you mean, he reminds you of the dick?"

I shrug. "The complete opposite of me: wealthy, sophisticated, but he does seem to be a good dad. All I know is that his boy is my daughter's best friend, and I would never want to do anything to ruin that."

"Well if he doesn't see how amazing you and Iris are, then you don't need him."

He carries her outside when we take our leave. He gets her buckled in, shuts the door, and then pulls me into his arms for a tight hug.

Once we get home, I'm able to direct my little, sleepy zombie into the house. In the bathroom I wash her face. In her bedroom I get her changed into her nightgown. After tucking her in, I step back so Peanut can hop up in bed with her. I turn on her nightlight and close the door.

I grab my phone as I sit on the sofa and send Joaquin a quick text.

Mona: Thank you again for coming to Iris' party. Is Max knocked out? Iris didn't even

wake up when I walked her sleepy butt into the house. ☺

I set my phone down and grab a glass of wine and settle on the sofa. I look at my phone and see that my text has been read, but no response. What did I expect, though? So what? We barely kissed. Maybe he was just grateful that I was sweet to his boy.

I turn on Parks and Rec on Netflix and drink my wine as I continuously look down at my phone that stays silent. Of course, that's for the best.

MONA

Iris runs ahead of my sisters and me. We decided to surprise her with a last hurrah weekend before school starts, and we booked a couple rooms at the Ritz-Carlton on Lake Oconee. My sisters were on board with that plan, but unfortunately, Miles is on a major deadline with his publisher, so there was no way he could come.

It's been almost a week since Iris' party, and I haven't heard from Joaquin. I'm not surprised, though, and I'll admit it stings a little. Luckily, Max has still been chatting with Iris almost every night.

I shake off the thoughts of Joaquin and hurry to catch my overly excited daughter as she makes her way toward the infinity pool. "Iris, wait for us," I holler after her.

She puts the brakes on and skids to a stop. My sister Sierra slides her arm through mine. "Have you seen the smorgasbord of hot men. My God, I'm in desperate need of dick."

"Oh my God. I can't believe you said that," I whisper harshly.

Sierra bumps my hip with hers. "Oh come on; lighten up. I think you're in desperate need of it too."

We make it to some lounge chairs and set up camp. After we spread our towels around, I spray sunscreen all over Iris as she fidgets, ready to get in the water. Once she's ready, Heidi holds her hand out to Iris, and they take off for the water.

I spray myself down with sunscreen. I'm in the middle of spraying Greta down when I hear a little voice call my name. "Mona! Iris' mom, it's me, Max." I find my favorite little brown-haired boy followed by Joaquin looking sexy as fuck in red and white board shorts and a black sleevcless t-shirt.

They're followed by the tall, good looking, built blond who was with him that day at the restaurant.

"Hi, Maximum. How are you?"

The boy surprises me by hugging me around the waist. "Great. Where's Iris?"

I point to where she's stepping into the water. "She's getting into the pool." He lets go and moves to run in her direction, but I stop him. "Sunscreen first, buddy." Max lets me spray him, and when I ruffle his hair and tell him he's done, he takes off.

My girl screams as soon as she sees Max. The kid runs right into the pool, hugging my daughter. I feel Joaquin stop next to me. God, he smells delicious. "Well, this is a nice surprise." Just from his voice alone my nipples are hard now. "You obviously had the same idea as us. This is my buddy, Nick—Nick, this is Mona."

The huge blond shakes my hand, but he only has eyes for Sierra. I laugh as he lets go of my hand. He grabs Sierra's, and they walk off.

Greta leans in. "Umm... Is she safe with that guy?"

I look to Joaquin. "Is my sister safe with him?"

"Of course. We've been best friends since high school. He's a bit of a player, loud, and sometimes inappropriate, but he's really a good guy."

While Joaquin strips his sleeveless t-shirt off, I take a quick second to admire his body. He's all lean, sinewy muscle and tan skin that my lips crave to touch. I look away before he catches me, but my sister does. She starts mimicking humping the air, and I shoot her a look communicating I want her to stop.

Greta does, but only when he turns back toward us. "Are you getting in the water?" He looks at me expectantly. "Mona?"

Oh God, was I just staring at him? "Umm... I'm sorry. Yes."

Joaquin takes the bottle from me, turns me around, and sprays the back of me, which I already did, but I'm not going to complain. My sister watches us with a raised brow. I mouth, "Stop it."

He hands it back to me.

I tuck the bottle into the tote bag I brought and then walk to the pool with Greta and Joaquin and find Iris and Max teaming up, splashing poor Heidi whose hot pinked-tipped hair hangs in her face.

"Iris, quit splashing your aunt." Both kids decide that I need to be wet, so they charge me.

I'm not sure how long we're playing in the

water, but Greta and Heidi ditched us to lay out, and now I'm sitting on the side of the pool watching Joaquin throw his son and my daughter into the water, over and over. The look of pure joy on Iris' face warms me.

I have no clue where Sierra and Nick went, and I'm sure I don't want to know what they're doing as well. Hopefully, they had enough sense to go back to his room, unless Max and Joaquin are staying with him, then they better take a couple cold showers.

Speaking of cold showers—I'm going to need one after watching Joaquin's sexy ass muscles bunch and contract as he picks the kids up and tosses them. My eyes have drifted multiple times to that damn V that goes down into his board shorts.

His tan skin glistens, and I know it begs for me to kiss and lick it. Ugh… I need to stop thinking about licking, kissing, or sucking anything on him. I need to remember that he reminds me too much of Iris' dad: wealthy, good looking, charismatic, very alpha and very much a heartbreaker.

"Hi." I hear a deep voice next to me. God, I was so lost in my thoughts about Joaquin I didn't notice the guy standing next to me.

I shield my eyes with my hand and look up. He's cute and has the boy next door kinda look. "Um… Hi."

"I'm Sean." He holds his hand out.

I place my hand in his. The least he could do is squat so we'd be sort of on the same level. "Mona."

"Are you here alone?"

Before I can answer him, hands wrap around my

waist, lifting me into the water. I let out a surprise squeak as Joaquin and I hit the water. I turn my head and see Sean watch us and then turn and walk away.

I look up at Joaquin. "What was that for?"

He shrugs a shoulder and lets me go. "You seemed uncomfortable, so I was rescuing you. You're welcome," he says while walking away from me and back toward the kids.

We let the kids play a little longer before helping them out and leading them over to our loungers. Joaquin and I work like we've been working together forever. I dry the kids off, and he helps them put their cover-ups on.

My sisters took off a while ago to eat lunch, leaving the four of us alone. I lead the kids toward a little spot for lunch that serves burgers, hot dogs, and other easy kid-friendly meals for two kids who're clearly winding down.

I hear a feminine voice behind us and turn to see a busty brunette in a tiny dress shamelessly flirting with Joaquin. The asshole smiles at her and seems to be eating it up. They talk quietly as I lead our kids to the counter to order.

Rationally I know I have no right to be jealous, but I want to rip the woman's extensions out and kick him in his balls. What's really pissing me off is that I've got his son with me, which I absolutely adore the little boy, but I'm not going to babysit while his dad bags himself a whore. Of course, that's not fair to call her that.

There's a small line, and I take the opportunity to ask the kids what they want. Max wants a cheeseburger and French fries, and my little vegetarian wants the grilled cheese and fresh fruit. I tell them to go grab a seat, and I'll order their food.

I feel *him* come up next to me, and I whisper heatedly, "I'm not your babysitter while you pick up women."

His deep chuckle irritates me. "She was coming on to me. She followed us from the pool." Joaquin looks behind us, and she's standing by a table with her phone to her ear, smiling at him.

Without thought I reach out, grabbing his hand, and lacing our fingers together. I shoot the brunette an irritated look, and that's all it takes for her to get the hint and disappear. We step up to the counter and I let go of his hand as he whispers, "Thanks. I had a feeling I wasn't going to be able to shake her."

"No worries." I look up at the girl behind the counter. "Hi, can I get a cheeseburger basket and a grilled cheese basket with Sprite for the drinks." I order a veggie and hummus wrap, and Joaquin orders a burger himself. I pull out some money, but he's already had her scan his phone to pay. "Here's for Iris and mine."

He shakes his head. "Nope, it's my treat for protecting me from that aggressive lady."

I throw my head back and laugh. "Yes, I'm sure you needed my protection from the scary lady."

Joaquin carries our drinks to the table. Iris looks like she's ready to fall asleep at the table, and Max looks the same.

After a quiet lunch, we head back to our rooms so the kids can nap. Before we head our separate ways, we make plans to take the kids for pizza and a couple games of bowling.

In our room, Iris immediately falls asleep, and since it's just us in here I lay down myself and fall asleep almost immediately.

This morning we're all meeting Joaquin, Nick, and Max for breakfast before they take us out on the lake to go tubing. Iris is looking forward to it so much she's been vibrating with excitement.

Last night, we all met to bowl and eat pizza. Even Sierra and Nick surfaced, but they were all over each other. I had to remind them that there were kids around. My sister would blush, bury her face in Nick's neck, and he would whisper, "Sorry."

I learned very quickly that the big blond behemoth was a really nice guy, even though he was loud and inappropriate. Max and Iris would climb him, and he'd just laugh and let them. My sisters were smitten with both men, and it was very irritating how they'd giggle at anything they said.

Sierra and Nick disappeared the moment we were finished. Then Heidi and Greta disappeared, leaving Joaquin, the kids, and me alone. We played some arcade games, and I watched as women shamelessly followed us around, flirting with him repeatedly.

When we finished, like true gentlemen they walked us to our hotel room. It didn't take long before my daughter and I both passed out.

"Mommy?"

I focus back on the present and turn to my daughter. "Yeah, honey?"

"I'm so excited to go tubing today. This has been the best weekend ever." She throws her arms around my waist, hugging me tightly.

"I'm so glad, honey. Can you go brush your teeth and put your sandals on?" She nods and then disappears into the bathroom.

I've got towels, sunscreen, and sunglasses in our beach bag. On top of my head is my favorite purple and white Sugar and Spice, Ink trucker hat. Nothing like a little self-promotion while we're out.

Iris comes out, and we're both in the same white cotton cover-up. The only difference is her trucker hat is baby blue and white. We head downstairs and spot Nick with Sierra in his lap by the front doors.

"Hey, guys," I call out. They stand as we approach. Iris runs to my sister, giving her a hug. "Where are Greta and Heidi?" I look around and don't see them.

"Greta texted me while Nick and I were eating breakfast. They stayed out late last night, so they were going back to bed, and later, they're going to lounge at the pool."

Max and Joaquin show up a few minutes later, and the six of us head through the hotel and down the path to the docks. Joaquin and Nick head inside the little building at the front. I lean into Sierra while we wait. "What's up with you and Nick?"

My sister started dating when she was sixteen and was always in a relationship. In college she had a serious boyfriend who broke her heart, and since then she hasn't really dated anyone.

66

She looks in the direction of the building he went into then turns back to me. "He is something else. The man has so much stamina, and I had to finally threaten bodily harm just to get a break. He's a restaurateur and said that anytime we want to eat at one of his restaurants, I just need to call, and he'll save us a table."

Sierra shrugs. "I like him, but this is just sex—fun, hot, incredibly intense sex."

We're going to have to discuss this more when we're alone. Joaquin and Nick come toward us, and Nick goes right to my sister, wrapping his arm around her waist and whispering in her ear. Hmmm… I'll be interested to see how that whole thing plays out.

Joaquin stops in front of me. "Are you ready? The boat is gassed up, and tubes are pumped up."

"Yep, I think we are."

He leads us toward the docks and to a gorgeous and expensive looking boat. "Wow, is this yours?"

"No, it's a rental. It's too much of a hassle to own a boat. I'd rather just rent and be done with it." He hops on the boat and then reaches for both kids, lifting them effortlessly inside.

Joaquin holds out his hand to me and then helps me step on. I quickly spray both kids with sunscreen and help them put their lifejackets on. I find Joaquin watching me with a strange look on his face.

"Are you okay?" I move toward him.

He shakes his head. "I'm fine, sorry. Thank you for getting Max ready." Nick and Sierra climb on, and Joaquin turns to the side and starts unwinding the ropes that hold the boat to the dock. He and

Nick push us off, and then he gets situated, starts the boat, and we slowly make our way away from the dock.

Once we're far enough from the dock, Joaquin increases his speed and both kids squeal. Sierra smiles at me as we make our way across the lake. What a way to end Iris' summer vacation.

MONA

I stare at the check in my hand like at any moment it's going to disappear. Sam actually followed through with something he said he was going to do. I certainly wasn't expecting a check in the amount of a thousand dollars, but I will take it. Iris and I have always lived comfortably—we're not rolling in it by any means, but she's well taken care of.

This money will be split: half to go into a savings account for my daughter, and I won't touch it unless we absolutely need to. The other half will go toward things my growing daughter needs.

Does this mean he's going to want visitation, sooner rather than later? I know I should be happy that Iris' father wants to spend time with her, to get to know her, but he hasn't wanted her until now—why?

I won't worry until I have a reason to. Since Iris is at school, I head to the bank and open a savings account for her, get groceries, and get her some art supplies.

School has been in session for two weeks, and things are good. Iris loves her teacher and has her friends from last year, but I know my daughter is missing her buddy, Max. They've been video chatting almost every night, or talking on the phone, but they desperately want to see each other. I need to talk to Joaquin about setting up a playdate.

I hate to admit it, but I miss spending time with Joaquin too. Our weekend in Lake Oconee had been such an amazing time. My daughter was always included in their antics, and when Iris was too scared to tube by herself, Joaquin was the one to take her out.

While Nick drove them around, I took a video of them, and my daughter had the biggest smile on her face. After we finished, we all went out for dinner, and Nick and Joaquin refused to let us pay. Sierra and Nick disappeared shortly after, and we took the kids to play mini golf.

It was grown-ups against the kids, and we "lost". By the time we got home Sunday evening, we were both exhausted and crashed after a couple grilled cheeses.

I head to work after I finish my errands. Office work is the part of my job I hate the most. It has to be done, and my sisters all voted me the lucky winner. I step inside and find our part-time receptionist dusting. "Hey, Jen. How are you?"

"I'm good, Mona. Do you have anything that you want me to do today?" I wish she could work for us more than she does, but she's got family commitments that keep her time limited.

I look around the studio. "You can check inventory and then maybe send out the reminder texts for upcoming appointments." The text option was such a good investment. I definitely think it's easier for us to reach the clients to confirm their appointments.

"Okay great, I'll get started." She grabs the order form and heads into the back. The chime above the door will alert Jen when someone walks in.

I wave at Greta and Heidi as I pass by and head into the office. After I boot up my laptop, I pay some bills. I update our newsletter with whose books are open for appointments. After that, I go through emails.

"Hard at work, I see." I freeze and look up to find Sam standing in the doorway. "Can I come in?"

"Uh… Yeah. Come on in." I stand and come around my desk. "I got the check. Thank you."

He sits on the loveseat, and I sit on the chair across from him. "Oh good. I wanted to ask you about setting up visitation. I'd like to get to know my daughter."

I wipe my sweaty palms on my thighs. "Okay. I think we should start small. She's never met you and doesn't know you."

Sam nods. "I agree. Maybe the three of us could have lunch and then go from there? I don't want to make her uncomfortable. Tawny and Nixon can wait until the next visit to meet her." Tawny was who he was with the first time I'd seen him after I had Iris.

"I'd appreciate that. I'll talk to her beforehand and explain things."

"Am I interrupting?" I look up and find Joaquin standing in the doorway.

I signal him to come in. "What are you doing here?"

Joaquin holds up a gift bag. "Max wanted Iris to have this." I take it, but don't look inside, although I'm dying to know what that precious boy bought for my daughter.

Sam stands. "This is Iris' father, Sam Brown. Sam, this is Joaquin Pena." I look at Sam. "I'll call you to set up a lunch with her."

"Okay, great." He looks between the two of us and then takes off.

Neither of us speaks at first. My head starts pounding, and I sift my fingers through my hair. "Is Iris close to her dad?"

I shake my head and laugh bitterly. "She's never met him. He bailed the moment the test came back positive."

He leads me to the loveseat and sits next to me. "What's he doing now?"

I tell him about my run-in with Sam, his desire to know his daughter, and that he's paid child support for the first time today. He looks pissed, and I don't know why that tickles me—I know it's just on Iris' behalf, but still.

Joaquin shakes his head. "Max hardly sees his mom. We were divorced by the time he was two, and I've always had primary custody. He cut into her social life. Max only sees her about once or twice a year, and it's hard. I don't like sharing him with her, and I don't know how good of care she takes of him. Every time he goes with her and

72

comes back, he's upset and not his normal, happy self."

He rests his elbows on his knee. "I know how it feels, and it's hard, but hopefully this will be a good experience for Iris."

"Thank you. I was hoping that he'd forget about her and disappear again, but you're right; this could be good for her." I grab his hand. "I'm sorry Max's mom doesn't have much to do with him. He's an amazing boy. You should be very proud."

He turns toward me, and before I know what's happening his lips are on mine. They feel even better than I've imagined. My fingers sift through his incredibly soft hair, but all too soon he pulls back. "Thank you for saying that."

"I said it because it's true. You're a good dad, Joaquin."

"And you're a great mom." This time I kiss him. I lick the seam of his lips until he opens to me. A moan rips from my throat the moment his tongue touches mine. I shift until I'm straddling his lap. Joaquin grips my hips, holding me tightly to him.

Just as I sink farther into the kiss, he ends it and lifts me off of him, gives a muttered goodbye, and is gone before I can react.

I come unstuck, jumping up from the couch, and I'm pissed. He can't treat me like this—kiss me one minute and then take off the next. Joaquin owes me answers, and I'm going to get them. With a quick Google search, I find his address and see he lives in the Buckhead District. He's got money, so of course he lives in a fancy neighborhood.

I've got one appointment today, and once I'm

finished I'm heading there and giving him a piece of my mind.

Three hours later I'm heading toward Joaquin's. My GPS has me turn down a winding driveway, and when his home comes into view I'm in awe. It's huge but beautiful and homey. It looks like a giant cottage with lots of windows surrounded by dark gray shutters; I bet the natural light is just stunning in there.

I shake it off, though, because I'm ticked. I climb out of my car and march toward his front door. As soon as I press the doorbell I hear a dog barking; again, I'm surprised he's got one. Through the beveled glass in the door, I see a figure moving toward it, and it's definitely female.

My heart beats rapidly when a beautiful brunette with lightly tanned skin opens the door. Awesome, he kissed me and then came home to this woman who is clearly more in his league. "Can I help you?"

Ugh, even her voice is gorgeous and all sultry too. "I-uh... I'm... Actually, never mind."

I back away and then turn as I hustle down the steps. "Wait!" she calls and then, "Max, get your dad. Mona's here."

I stop and turn toward her. "I'm Victoria, Joaquin's cousin," she says and ends in a giggle.

I'm so embarrassed right now, but I slowly make my way back to her when Max comes tearing out of the house followed by a little dog. "Mona! Did you come to see me? Where's Iris, did she get her present?"

I squat in front of him. "Hey, Maximum. I came to see your dad, and Iris is with her uncle. She'll get her present when I get home." He hugs me and pulls back while the little white fluff ball jumps all over me. I pick up the dog, and it proceeds to lick my face. "Who is this?"

"That's Fluffy."

I hold up the dog so we look eye to eye. "Well hello, Fluffy."

I look up and find Joaquin walking toward us. He's in jeans and a t-shirt and looks hot as usual. "Max, why don't you go into the house. I need to talk to Mona."

Max surprises me by placing a kiss on my cheek before taking the dog from me. Once he and the dog go inside, Joaquin comes toward me with a smirk on his face.

"What?" I ask and shake my head. "I'm such a dork, and I'm sorry I just showed up here. That kiss was intense, and then you just left. If you're not interested, just tell me because you act like you are, but then act like you aren't." I'm not sure where this bravery is coming from, but I'm glad it showed up.

"Don't be sorry. I'm glad you did, and I'm sorry I've been giving you mixed signals. I don't want or need a relationship, but I'm drawn to you. I like spending time with you." He rubs a hand over the top of his head.

"I don't want a relationship either." He seriously has heartbreaker written all over him. The same way Sam did, and I don't dare repeat that.

"What if we just had sex, a friend with benefits situation? No muss, no fuss; our kids can spend time together because that's what they want, and you and I can scratch an itch without things getting ...

complicated."

I shake my head. "Every romance I've read—every movie I've seen—this sort of arrangement almost always ends badly." I've never been one for casual sex. Could I sleep with someone without my heart getting involved?

"We won't let it end badly."

That's easier said than done. I step toward him. "Our kids care about each other so much. What if we end up hurting them?"

Joaquin grabs my face in his large hands. "We'll just have to make sure we don't." He kisses me chastely before stepping back. "Let me take you to dinner this weekend. We'll talk. You can bring Iris over, and Victoria can watch them."

"Okay, and I'll give you my answer then."

He nods once. "Great, we'll talk this week."

I nod. "Sure. I better go, I have to pick up Iris at Miles'."

Joaquin walks me to my driver's side door. He opens it for me, and I climb in. Grabbing the top of the door, he leans in. "Can I just say that I find it so adorable that you got jealous when my cousin answered the door." With that, he shuts the door.

He walks in front of my car, and I give my horn a quick little beep. Joaquin looks at me, and I give him the finger. He throws his head back and laughs.

On my way home his proposition goes through my mind over and over. I've only had sex twice since Iris was born, and they were good ... I guess. Joaquin looks like he'd blow my mind. He moves with purpose, but sensuously, if that even makes sense.

In his swim trunks, I hadn't missed the bulge, the very large bulge. Ugh … I need Sierra. I hit the Bluetooth on my steering wheel, and Sierra's voice comes through the speakers. "Hey, girl. I heard Sam and Joaquin were both at the studio today. How the fuck did that go?"

"I'll give you the Cliffs Notes version. I got a thousand dollar check from Sam for child support, and he showed up today, hoping to set up some time to get to know Iris. I told him we'd start with lunch, and he promised it would be just the three of us until my girl was comfortable." I pick up my bottle of water and take a sip.

"Ugh … I hate him. Why couldn't he have dropped off the face of the earth? Now, how does Joaquin fit into all this?"

"He stopped by with a gift for Iris from Max."

"Oh my God, I love that little guy."

I smile as she says it because I really do too. "I know, right. Anyway, after Sam left, we started talking. He told me about Max's mom, and basically she sees him once or twice a year. He was just being sweet, and I told him he was a good dad, and then he kissed me." I then tell her that he split, and I showed up at his house.

Sierra is laughing hysterically.

"I don't find this funny. I made a fool out of myself. What's worse is that she knew who I was, but that's not why I called." I take a deep breath. "Joaquin doesn't want a relationship, and honestly, I don't either. He says he's drawn to me, and we're both attracted to each other. Well, he suggested that we have a friends with benefits sort of situation. I told…"

Sierra interrupts me. "Do it. Get the cobwebs out of your hoo-ha, and fuck that beautiful man."

"Our kids are best friends. What if this ends badly, which these situations seem to only end that way? It could hurt our kids in the process."

"Stop with what-ifs, and have some fun. You deserve to cut loose, and if you get to sample some of that man candy then that's just a bonus. I'm getting horny on your behalf."

I roll my eyes. "Control yourself. We're going to have dinner this weekend. I'm taking Iris to his house, and his cousin will watch the kids."

"Okay, this week you need to go get a wax, a mani, and a pedi and a really good massage so you aren't so tense when you finally get … it … on."

"I'm hanging up now."

Just as I press the button to disconnect, I hear her shout, "Wax your bush!"

As I drive toward my brother's place, I do it smiling.

"Just keep the plastic wrap on it until you get home, wash it with antibacterial soap, and pat dry with a towel. Then put a thin layer of a fragrance-free, alcohol-free lotion on it." I hand her a card. "These are the ones that we recommend."

I walk her to the counter and ring her up. She signs my iPad and says goodbye. "Call us if you have any questions."

After wiping off my station, I pull out my phone

and see that I have a text from Joaquin. Our date is tonight, and I've been a nervous wreck all week. I've bought six different dresses, trying to find the right one. I know my style is a little different than his, and I don't want to embarrass him.

Sam used to chastise me on my style. I'm confident in my style, but I know what men like Sam and Joaquin expect from their women. I'm sure Joaquin's ex-wife looks like a supermodel and the type worthy to be on his arm.

Ugh... I hate when I get all negative. If he can't accept me for who I am then I don't need him. That's one thing I've always tried to teach my daughter—to be proud of who she is and don't let anyone try to change that.

The night I agreed to have dinner with him, I had gotten home with Iris and watched as she tore the paper out of the gift bag and screamed. They bought her a sketch pad, fancy color pencils, and a little messenger bag to carry everything in.

I took a picture of her holding up all of her goodies and sent it to Joaquin. "Mommy, I need your phone. I *have* to call Max and tell him thank you."

Iris took my phone and hit Joaquin's number. I heard his deep voice as he answered. "Hi, Joaq. This is Iris. Can I talk to Max, please? It's very, very important." I smiled at my girl because she was just so sweet. "Thank you."

The minute Max got on the phone, Iris started talking a mile a minute and headed down the hall to her room. While they were talking, I straightened up the kitchen and started dinner. I made us tofu tacos with black beans, lettuce, avocado, and pico de gallo.

Sometimes it's so hard being vegetarians surrounded by meat eaters, but Iris and I have managed pretty well. Of course, she could decide to eat meat tomorrow, and I'd be okay with that.

She came out about a half hour later. "He had to have a shower, but he says I get to come to his house. Is that true?"

"Yeah, baby. Joaquin and I are going to have dinner, and he thought you might want to see Max."

Iris hopped up and down, squealing.

The rest of the week went by fast, but that was only because I kept busy and tried not to think about what I was going to agree too—because yes, I was going to engage in a friend with benefits situation with Joaquin.

I also took my sister's advice and went and got waxed, which was freaking painful. I got my nails and toes done. The only thing I didn't do was get a massage. Instead, I opted to just do my craptastic yoga and meditate.

Before Iris, I wasn't into yoga or meditation. Sometimes I ran or did kickboxing, but after Iris, I had some postpartum depression. My doctor and I talked about things I could do day to day besides the medication she put me on.

She suggested the yoga, and once I'd been doing that for a while the instructor told me about meditating, and that was all she wrote.

I'm not even sure we will have sex this weekend, but I am as prepared as I'm going to be.

Now I try on this adorable gray sheath dress that

hits me right above my knees. It hugs my curves and compliments them. The sleeves are capped, and my ink is on full display. I look at myself in my full-length mirror and turn every which way.

I can't take too much longer, or we're going to be late, so I decide that this is the dress I'm going to wear. In my closet, I grab my black wedge sandals. Once I've got them on, I spritz some of my perfume into the air and walk through it twice.

I grab my light pink gloss and dab it on my lips. I've left my lavender locks down tonight in sleek, shiny sheets. I throw on the black pearl bracelet my parents gave to me when I turned eighteen, which goes well with the black diamond studs in my ears.

Iris comes tearing into the room. "Mom, you look so pretty. Is Joaq your boyfriend? Are you going to get married and make Max my brother? I hope so."

"Slow down, girlfriend. Mom doesn't have a boyfriend, and she's not getting married. Do you want Max to be your brother?"

She flops down on my bed and sighs dramatically. "Well duh … he's only my best friend in the entire world, and I love him, but like a brother. He loves me like a sister."

Well, who could argue with that logic?

JOAQUIN

"*Te ves guapo*," Victoria announces from the doorway.

I nod while I adjust my shirt before slipping my suit jacket on. "I know I look handsome." She rolls her eyes as I grab my watch and put it around my wrist. "I appreciate you looking after the kids. I'm not sure how tonight is going to go."

"It's no problem, *primo*. We're going to order pizza, no meat for Iris, and we're going to have ice cream and watch some movies. You ... do whatever." She turns on her heel and disappears out of my room.

I grab my phone and wallet and head out into the living room where Max is sitting in front of the window, waiting for Iris and Mona to get here.

Max jumps up and flies toward the door. "They're here!" I follow sedately behind him. From the doorway, I watch Max practically tackle Iris after she climbs out of the car, and then hand in hand they run past me into the house.

"Hello, Iris," I call out to the little blonde running with my son.

"Hi, Joaq!"—which is pronounced like walk— "Thanks for letting me see Max."

I turn back to the doorway and find Mona walking toward me. Fuck, I can feel my dick getting hard right now.

The woman is a vision; that dress looks like it was designed specifically for her. Her colorful ink is on full display. Before I met Mona and her sisters, I never really considered tattoos attractive on women, but I've had to reevaluate those thoughts because they're all gorgeous.

Her lavender hair is super straight, shiny, and even more vibrant. "Wow. You look amazing."

Mona's cheeks turn pink. "Thanks. You're not so bad yourself." She looks up at me smiling. "If you didn't notice, the kids were very happy to see each other."

"Clearly. Come on in, and I'll give you a tour." She steps inside, and I close the door behind her. I lead her through the living room, kitchen/dining room. Mona oohs and aahs while running her hand along the granite countertop on the kitchen island.

I lead her upstairs to Max's room, and we find the kids playing video games. "Max, I want you on your best behavior tonight. Help Iris if she needs anything, and be good for Victoria, okay?"

"Okay, Dad. Hi, Mona."

"Hey, Maximum. You and Iris have fun tonight." They both give us a wave, not even stopping their game playing. "Bye, sweetheart."

I lead her downstairs with a hand on the small of her back. Inconspicuously I inhale the light fruity scent she's wearing, but all it does is make me hungry for her. More than anything I'd love to bury my nose in her neck and get even closer to her scent.

We find Victoria in the kitchen with Fluffy in her arms. "I thought I should have him outside when you first got here. I didn't want him jumping on you." She eyes Mona's outfit. "You look great. Oh ... I wanted to ask; I know Iris doesn't eat meat, but are there any vegetables she doesn't eat?"

"When you order pizza, you can order her the garden; she likes all of the veggies on that. I'm sorry that you have to order special for her." She holds up her purse. "Let me get you some money."

I put my hand on her arm to stop her from rifling through her purse. "You're not paying for her pizza. I invited you to dinner and asked you to bring your daughter. It's my treat."

Mona lets out a little huff. "Okay, but I'll get next time. Thank you for keeping an eye on her, Victoria. She's a good girl and will listen."

"It's my pleasure. Now you kids go have fun. Don't do anything I wouldn't do."

I roll my eyes at my cousin because she loves being a pain in the ass. Of course, she was going to try to embarrass me. Too bad I'm a thirty-year-old man who doesn't embarrass easily.

Mona's quiet as we head outside to my Range Rover. I open her door and help her inside. "Where are we going?" she asks as I climb in the driver's side.

"We're going to Bacchanalia. Have you been?"

She shakes her head. "No, but I hear it's amazing. It's not really in my price range," Mona says the last part quietly.

I reach out grabbing her hand. "Well, you're in for a treat, and I'm glad I get to be the one to introduce you to the amazing food they have."

The silence at first is awkward, which is new to me. I've always been a very confident man and have always had good luck with the ladies. It's always been easy finding women to share my bed. Conversation was always easy, generic, but with her, I don't want generic because that's not who she is—she's special.

Thankfully, she's the first to speak. "Iris has been drawing up a storm since she got the sketch pad and colored pencils. That was really sweet of you guys to do that for her." Mona surprises me by placing her hand over mine as I rest it on my thigh.

"Iris doesn't have a lot of friends. If you haven't noticed my girl loves to talk, sing, and dance. She does it everywhere, and kids being kids think it's weird, and sometimes it makes kids think twice before spending time with her. Iris says that Max is her friend because he likes her no matter what."

She's smiling at me in a way that makes me want to kiss her hard. "I've been lucky. He's truly an amazing kid. I grew up with nannies because my parents were always too busy to raise a child; my dad with work and Mom with her social calendar. My parents spoiled me with things, not love. I never intended to have children. I didn't want to continue that cycle. When I found out Max was coming, I swore we were going to do it right." I squeeze her hand.

"My ex hired a nanny, and I fired her immediately. His mom never got up with him; I did. He flipped my world upside down, but I wouldn't change any of it. I fought her tooth and nail for custody; I ended up paying her fifteen grand cash to agree to me having full custody. From the start, my son only had me. Victoria moved in, thankfully, to help because she was raised the same way as me, and she wanted to give him so much more than what we had."

Where did all of that just come from? I'm not usually a sharer—especially with a woman, but maybe she's the right person to talk to about this because I don't want generic conversation; I want something real. "Sorry, I don't know why I just told you all of that. Victoria and Nick are the only ones I really talk to about that kind of stuff."

"Well, we are friends, and friends talk about stuff that matters. Hell, I unloaded on you about Iris' dad the other day. You are really a good Dad, and you and I both know that being a single parent isn't easy, but we are both lucky to have family members who help."

I pull into the parking lot of Bacchanalia and park. After helping Mona out of my Rover, with a hand to the small of her back, I lead her inside. At the hostess stand, I give the woman my name and don't miss the way she looks me up and down.

I also don't miss the snarky look she gives Mona. The girl is obviously jealous because Mona is a knockout, and in that dress—the hair, the makeup, and her confidence—she's even more of one.

We're led to a table by the window, giving us a prime view of downtown. Our waiter appears, and I order a scotch and soda, and Mona orders a glass of wine. Once he drops our drinks off and takes our order, I lean slightly forward. "Have you thought about my proposition?"

She takes a healthy sip from her glass. "I have."

I'm dying to know if she's going to go through with it. I take a large drink and set my glass down, trying to appear casual. "Oh yeah. What are you thinking?"

"If we do this, there can't be any other women."

I nod. "Okay and no other men."

"Agreed. If at any time you want to end it, I just ask that you have the decency to tell me straight up, and I'll do the same. Especially since neither of us is looking for a relationship. The last thing, and most important, is if this starts to affect either of our kids negatively then we break it off." She drains her glass of wine. "I do have one question."

"Okay, let me have it."

"Why me? You're obviously a good looking man. You could probably have any woman you want, and I'm sure you probably have."

I think of my words carefully. "Why not you? Mona, I'm very attracted to you—in a way I haven't been attracted to another woman in a long time." I might as well put it all out there. "I'm drawn to you, and I can't explain it, but the idea of touching every inch of your body makes my heart race. You're intoxicating."

Her teeth sink into her bottom lip, and her cheeks

turn a dark shade of pink. "Does that make you uncomfortable?" I ask as I reach across the table, grabbing her hand.

Mona shakes her head. "Not at all."

"Good." Our waiter brings our first course, breaking the moment.

She smiles down at the plate in front of her and then gives me a smile that makes my heart beat funny. "Let's dig in," I tell her before doing just that.

Each course they bring, me and every other man in this place can't keep our eyes off of Mona while she eats. She's so expressive and enjoying every bite of her food. I'll admit, for it being vegetarian it looks really good.

Once we finish dessert, I pay the check. I help Mona up from her chair and wrap my arm around her waist; I smile when I feel her arm wrap around mine. Outside, I lead her to the Rover. "Do you want to go have a drink or coffee before we head back to the house?"

She's quiet for a moment, and then she looks up at me. "We could go back to my place for a drink."

"Okay." She gives me her address when I climb in the SUV.

I pull up in front of a cute little craftsman home. The siding is a dark gray with navy blue shutters and white trim. There's a swing on the porch and two Adirondack chairs that I can just imagine Mona and Iris sitting in.

I climb out and come around to her side to help her down. For the first time since I was a teenager, my nerves assail me as I follow behind her up the steps. She unlocks the door, and I grab it, holding it open for her to step inside. I follow close behind, locking the door behind me.

The only thing I get to notice is the walls are covered in pictures of Iris and Mona and even some of her and her sisters.

Mona comes over and stands next to me. "As you can see I've had *many* different hair colors."

"You were still beautiful."

She turns to me and grabs my face, pulling it down to hers. She kisses me softly, chastely at first, but I let her control the pace for a minute, and then I have to take over. I grab a handful of her hair, using it to tip her head back and deepening the kiss.

She opens to me, and when my tongue brushes hers, I groan. Fuck, she tastes good. I can still taste the hint of chocolate soufflé on her tongue. My hands glide down her back until I reach her luscious ass. I pull her into me, letting her feel my massive erection.

Mona grabs the lapels of my jacket, pushing it off my shoulders and down my arms. She reaches between us and pulls my shirt from my pants. I reach the zipper at the back of her dress.

The sound of the zipper going down echoes in the room, and I grab the sleeves and pull it down. I have to see her, so I reluctantly pull away from her. God, she's perfection in the little scraps of black lace, and she looks even sexier than she did in her bikinis.

With quick hands, I unbutton my shirt and pull it off—followed by my undershirt. I don't miss the way she stares at my bare chest, licking her lips.

Mona's eyes drift to my dick, which feels like it's about to punch a hole through my pants.

"Bedroom?" I say, my voice hoarse.

She grabs my hand and pulls me down the hall to her bedroom. I pick her, turn her, and press her into the wall as I kiss her hard. I move down her neck, licking and nipping every inch of her skin.

"You smell like heaven," I whisper against her skin. I don't miss the goose bumps that pop up all over her body.

I grab her ass, lifting her higher, and it puts her tits right in my face. "Take them out." She grips the top of her strapless bra, pulling the cups down until her dark pink nipples are revealed to me.

I lean in, sucking one tip into my mouth. Her arms wrap around my head, holding me to her breasts as she cries out. I switch to the other, giving it the same treatment. I'm so fucking turned on by her mewls and cries.

I carry her to bed, climbing onto it with her still wrapped around me. Her lavender hair spreads out around her. I push up on my forearm. "You're absolutely stunning. Lift up for me."

Mona wraps her arms around my back, lifting her upper body so I can reach behind her and unhook her bra. She lays back, and I sit up on my knees, looking her over. I'm a lucky fucking man.

I grab her panties and work them down her legs before climbing off of her bed and grabbing a condom from my wallet after shucking my pants and boxer briefs. Mona pushes herself up, resting on her elbows. Her eyes immediately go to my throbbing dick, and he definitely likes the attention.

Her tongue peeks out, running back and forth across her lush lower lip.

I toss the condom on the bed, and then I grab Mona by the ankles, spreading her legs wide. "I can't wait to taste your hot little cunt. Do you want me to taste you?"

Mona nods, lifting her hips to me. "Yes … please."

I bend down, my breath hitting her wet folds in warm puffs. She squirms, and I can see that she's very wet. The first swipe of my tongue through her pussy and Mona's hips jerk up off the bed.

I suck her clit into my mouth as I grip both breasts, tweaking her nipples with each pull. Mona's fingers grip my hair as I lick her pussy again, moaning as her spicy, sweet flavor hits my tongue.

I work one finger inside her—God, she's tight. While sucking on her clit, I ease the one finger out then work two inside her. I scissor them, stretching her a little to accommodate my size. She's so wet that she's drenching my hand. I turn my fingers and tickle the little spot inside of her that drives women wild.

While I work that spot, I press down on the spot above her pubic bone. I look up at her, and she lets go of my hair and grabs the slats of her headboard, arches her back, and cries incoherently. "Come for me, baby. Let me hear you let go."

I bend down, nip her clit, and she detonates—drenching my hand as she cries out over and over. When she finishes coming, I pull my fingers from her and lick her juices off my fingers. As she pants, she grabs my hand then proceeds to suck my fingers into her hot mouth.

My cock is leaking pre-cum all over her, and it aches to be inside her. I grab her arms, pinning them above her head. "Are you ready to get fucked?" I let go of her hands.

"Mmm hmm." She grabs the condom, ripping it open with her teeth. She pulls it out, but I pluck it from her fingers. "If you touch me right now, I'm going to come."

I make quick work of sheathing myself and then grab my dick, rubbing it through her arousal. Mona's eyes hold mine as I line my dick up with her entrance. Inch by inch I work myself inside of her. Her pussy is so tight, and the desire to come hits me, but I try to think of anything to keep myself from coming.

When I'm halfway in, I pull almost all the way out before thrusting in to the hilt. Mona cries out, and I lean down kissing her lips. I flex my hips and thrust back in. She moans against my lips. "Please fuck me."

That's all I need to hear before thrusting into her, deep and hard. "You feel so good," I say as I grab her behind one thigh, lift it higher, and open her more to me, and I swear I sink further inside her.

When she begins to come, she squeezes me so tight. I grab the headboard for leverage and pound into her at a punishing pace. I sink into her once, twice, and hold myself snuggly inside her as I come so hard I see stars.

I brush a lock of her hair out of her face. "I didn't hurt you, did I?"

Mona leans up, kissing then nipping my chin. "You didn't hurt me."

"Good. Let me get rid of the condom, and I'll be right back." I kiss her lip and pull my softening cock from her. In the bathroom, I wrap my condom up and throw it in the trash. I wash my hands and then head into the bedroom. I hope to crawl in bed with her for a bit before we have to head back.

I just don't expect to find her already up and getting dressed. I come up behind her and wrap my arms around her. "What are you doing?"

I turn her in my arms, and she looks up at me. "I-I just thought since we're doing the whole friends with benefits thing that we shouldn't do anything that resembles a relationship. You know, so those lines don't get crossed."

I'm not sure if I like that. No, I'm not the biggest cuddler, but I don't want her thinking that this is a whole wham, bam, thank you, ma'am either. "You're right, but I still want to kiss those lips."

I tilt her chin up and kiss her. Once, twice, and a third before letting her go. She disappears into the hall. I get dressed and find her in the kitchen drinking a bottle of water. I take it from her and drink the rest of it before handing it back to her empty.

Mona holds it up. "Seriously? Butthead."

I wrap my arms around her, tickling her sides until she's gasping for breath and begging me to stop. Since when have I been a tickler except with Max? "Give me the grand tour?" I ask with my lips against her neck.

"Sure, it's not as nice as your place, though."

"Hey,"—I grab her forearm—"from what I've seen this is totally yours and Iris' style." She nods and leads me into the living room. I didn't notice earlier, but it's very soft and feminine. The walls are a warm taupe, her furniture is brown, but covered in colorful pillows and with a light purple blanket draped over the back.

A yoga mat and a big round pillow sit in the corner. The TV sets on a small entertainment center in the corner and is decorated with what looks like little pieces of pottery. "Iris made a lot of these," she says, her voice full of pride.

The girl is only seven, but it's clear she's got the artistic gene flowing through her veins.

Mona grabs my hand and leads me down the hall to a room decorated in pinks, purples, and unicorns. I smile because this room looks exactly like what I pictured. She's got pictures on the walls and posters. Her bookshelf is loaded with different books, and on her little desk are the art supplies we bought for her.

She surprises me by wrapping her arm around my waist. "You guys were so sweet to do that for her."

We finish the tour and make out on the couch for a while before we head back to my place so she can grab Iris.

While holding her hand in my SUV, I can't help but wonder how long I'm going to be able to keep to the friends with benefits because she's already got me wanting more.

MONA

While preparing the stencil for the tattoo I'm getting ready to do, I can't help but blush thinking about the past two weeks. I've always thought I had a healthy sex drive, but apparently, I've been wrong. With Joaquin, I can't seem to get enough.

We've been sneaking away for any chance to be alone. The first week it was him coming over during the lunch hour. This past week started with him showing up at the studio and locking the office door then taking me on the desk and then the loveseat. Then there was meeting him at his place as soon as I dropped Iris off at school the day before yesterday. My cheeks heat up thinking about it. That day things began to shift between us, or I felt like they did...

My stomach flips somersaults the moment I pull down Joaquin's road. This desperate need to see him is unfamiliar, but I welcome it although I know I should proceed with caution. I'm at risk of falling more so than I ever did with Sam, giving Joaquin the power to destroy me. I take a deep breath and park my car. In the rearview mirror, I give myself a once-over.

After smoothing my hair down, I grab my purse and climb out. I haven't even made it up the walkway before the door opens, and Joaquin stalks toward me in basketball shorts, shirtless. I let out a little squeak when he picks me up and throws me over his shoulder.

"Put me down, maniac." He slaps me on my ass. "Hey, what was that for?"

He says nothing, but he picks up the pace as he heads through his house. Once in his room, I sail through the air and land with a bounce on his bed. Joaquin follows me down. "I was beginning to think you were never going to get here."

I lean up and kiss his lips. "You're so impatient."

"I know, but I woke up so hard this morning." He kisses behind my ear; I love that. "I was just thinking about the blow job you gave me while I sat at your desk the other day."

"I was pretty amazing wasn't I?" I give him my sauciest wink. With quick hands, he strips off my shirt followed by my bra. Then, in one quick motion, my cut-off jean shorts and panties are gone.

"You have no idea how amazing you are," he says quietly, and it makes my heart flutter.

Joaquin strips out of his shorts, his hard cock bobbing as he crawls onto the bed. He grabs my ankles, spreads my legs wide, and pulls me closer to him. His brown eyes are so intense right now as he scans my body with his hungry gaze.

"Please tell me you're ready for me. Show me your pussy." I reach down with trembling hands and run my fingers through my arousal, moaning when I reach my clit. I close my eyes and arch my back as I rub it.

I open my eyes when he grabs my wrist. "I didn't tell you, you could touch yourself." My pussy spasms as he pulls my hand toward his mouth. Joaquin licks my arousal off each finger, moaning as he does it.

He grabs a condom from his bedside table and quickly dons it. "Flip over, baby, on your hands and knees."

I do as he says and feel him come between my legs. Joaquin leans over my back, kissing me between my shoulder blades, and then following the path of my spine with his lips and tongue.

Goose bumps pop up all over my body as he lightly blows on my heated flesh. He reaches between my legs and strokes my pussy until I'm a squirming, panting mess. "Joaquin, if you don't fuck me right now, I'm leaving." Of course, I'm not serious, but damn he's got me so on edge.

I yelp at the first slap of his hand on my ass. "What the hell!"

He swats me three more times, and I hate admitting that I like it ... too much, which is evident when Joaquin sticks his hand between my legs. "You're soaked."

I wiggle my ass, begging for his fingers, his cock—at this point, I'll take anything. I'm practically sobbing as I beg him to fuck me.

"Please, baby, I need you." I barely recognize my own voice.

Finally, I feel the head of his cock at the opening of my pussy. The moment he slides inside me I come so violently that I see stars. I push back against Joaquin as he grabs my hips and pounds into me at a punishing pace.

He reaches around and strums my clit until I come again. Joaquin follows behind me, burying himself to the hilt and pulsing inside of me. Our pants are the only sound that can be heard besides my heart beating in my ears.

He kisses the middle of my back and holds his lips there. I close my eyes and savor the feel of them. Joaquin pulls out of me, and I collapse. He removes the condom and then he rolls into me, wrapping his arms around me. I should pull away. I should climb out of his bed, get dressed, and leave.

Instead, I roll until we're chest to chest. "I should go," I whisper, but I don't make any attempt to get out of bed. It's like laying on a fluffy, yet firm cloud.

"Don't go, not yet." Joaquin brushes my hair out of my face. It's such a tender gesture it warms my heart. "Do you guys want to have dinner tonight? Maybe go out for pizza?"

I rub my thumb against the stubble of his chin. "Pizza sounds good."

He glides his hand up and down my side. "How did Iris do on her spelling test?"

I love that he asks about her. "She aced it. Max quizzed her over Facetime—Iris was extremely nervous about it until he worked with her."

Joaquin smiles and leans down, kissing me on the lips. "Atta girl. We'll go to Gino's and celebrate."

"That sounds yummy."

He hugs me to his chest. "Good. Then it's a date."

We make plans for him and Max to pick us up at Sugar and Spice later. I don't leave before we have a heavy make-out session at his front door. After kissing me senseless, he cups my cheek. "I look forward to having pizza with two of the most beautiful women in Atlanta later."

I swear my heart flutters at his words. He kisses me one more time, and I float all the way to my car.

"Mona? Mona—hello?" I turn back to my sister Sierra. "Are you okay? You kind of spaced out with a dreamy look on your face."

I shake my head, clearing the Joaquin fog from my brain. "Yeah, I'm fine; sorry. Did you need something?"

"No, just wanted to make sure you were okay." She leans in close. "Has Joaquin broken your brain with his good loving?"

I try to hide my surprise. We've tried to keep our non-relationship to ourselves. "I don't know what you're talking about." I avoid looking at her.

"I know you have a client waiting, but we will talk later about when Greta stopped by earlier this week and saw your car here along with a certain someone's Range Rover. She may have heard some strange noises coming from the office too."

My cheeks heat up immediately. I kept our arrangement to myself because it's strictly sex, and

I didn't want my nosy sisters to get the wrong idea about us.

I grab the stencil and take it over to my client who's been waiting patiently. "Sorry about that."

"No worries." While the stencil dries, I get everything ready. I grab a mint and pop it into my mouth. We're working on finishing up her sleeve today, and we'll probably go for at least a couple hours. She's always listening to audiobooks when I work, which is fine with me.

It cracks me up when she listens to them because every so often she'll laugh softly, or a tiny smile will grace her lips.

At two hours and ten minutes we're finally finished, and it looks incredible. It's a portrait of a cheetah that's on her bicep, but it's the details that took so long. I wanted to make it as realistic as I could. It's surrounded by orchids and vines.

I spray it and then wipe it down before letting her look at it. The smile that graces her lips fills me with pride. "Mona, you outdid yourself. It's gorgeous."

"Thank you, and I'm glad you love it." I cover it quickly and accept the hug that she gives me. She pays me and gives me a really nice tip. We exchange goodbyes, and I head to my office so I can grab my stuff, get Iris, and then head home.

My brother's on a deadline, so I told him to stay put instead of walking us down when I grab Iris. We pull up, and she climbs out and waits for me on the sidewalk. Peanut greets us at the door with a jaunty little meow. He follows Iris down the hall to her room.

She comes out with him in her arms a few minutes later. They sit on the floor, and she's playing with him when my phone rings. I look to see who is calling me and feel my stomach sink when Sam's name pops up.

"Sweetheart, I'm going to my room to take this call."

"Okay, Mom."

I hustle down the hall to my bedroom. "Hello, Sam."

"How are you, Mona? How's Iris?"

I pinch the bridge of my nose. "We're great. How are you?"

"Doing well. My father's finally made me partner. I know this is out of the blue, but I'd like to see if you and Iris want to meet for lunch tomorrow. I know it's not a lot of time, but I want us to get to know each other because we're having a party to celebrate the firm, and I'd like Iris to be there."

I close my eyes. "Um … sure, that's fine. Th-that's nice of you to include her." Why does talking to him turn me into the naïve young woman who fell for his charms and bullshit, but he did give me the greatest gift in the entire world.

"Great." He sounds relieved. "Where would you like to meet?"

"How about Herban Fix. That's Iris' favorite restaurant. We're vegetarians."

His chuckle irritates me. "Really? You've always *had* to be different."

Don't say anything; keep your mouth shut. I need to make sure I keep it friendly so he doesn't try to pull some shit. "Yep. I quit eating meat when she was a newborn, and she never has. If she decides to, I'm fine with that too."

"Okay, fine. We can go to Herban Fix. Let's meet at one o'clock; is that okay?"

I agree, and we hang up. Now it's time to explain to my daughter that she has a father, a father who now wants to see her. I pull up Joaquin's string of texts and shoot him a quick one.

Mona: Hey, will you be around to talk later? Sam just called, and Iris and I are meeting him for lunch tomorrow. ☹

The black dots bounce immediately.

Joaquin: Yes, are you okay with this?

Mona: Not okay, but if he's genuine then I'm happy for my daughter; although, I don't love the idea of sharing her.

It's quiet for a moment and then the dots bounce.

Joaquin: You've got this. Call me after she goes to bed.

Mona: Okay, thanks.

After I plug my phone into the charger, I take a deep breath, blow it out slowly, and head out to see my daughter.

I pull into the parking lot of the restaurant and shut the car off. I turn to look at my daughter in the backseat, and she looks so nervous.

Surprisingly, last night when we talked, she was very excited about the idea of having a dad. Iris asked me lots of questions about him, and I brushed off her questions about where he's been.

I called Joaquin after I finally got her to lay down, and he reminded me that as long as Sam wasn't an asshole that this was good for Iris. Before we hung up, he invited us over to help sample several dessert recipes that Victoria has been trying out.

After that, I called Heidi, because Greta and Sierra were still working, to tell her about lunch with Sam. Just because I knew she'd share with my other sisters. I'll tell Miles about it after it's done. Hopefully, it'll be a positive story.

This morning Iris made me do her hair and changed her outfit several times until she found the right one. She decided on a light pink maxi dress with a purple quarter sleeved cardigan with unicorns all over it and purple flip-flops.

I'm dressed very similar per her request. My maxi dress is a darker pink covered in white sugar skulls and black flip-flops on my feet.

We climb out of the car, and she slips her hand into mine. "Don't be nervous, sweetheart. Your dad is going to see right away what a special little girl you are."

Normally she's a chatterbox, but right now she's not saying much of anything. As soon as we step inside, I find Sam standing by the door holding a little gift bag. That man has always been cocky, arrogant, and self-confident.

Right now he looks nervous as hell. I decide to set a good example. "Hey, Sam. How are you?"

He leans down and kisses my cheek. "Hi, Mona. I'm good." Sam looks down at Iris. "Hi Iris, I'm Sam ... your dad."

Iris looks up at him and then up at me. I mouth, *"Go ahead."* I hold my breath, watching as Iris walks toward him and holds out her hand to him.

Sam takes hers and pumps it twice. "This is for you." He hands her the gift bag. "Should we get a table?" he asks.

"Yep," Iris says and smiles up at him.

He keeps ahold of Iris' hand as the hostess leads us to a table. At least he has manners still and pulls out Iris' chair as well as mine. Our waitress comes and takes our drink order and then leaves us.

Silence is awkward and uncomfortable at first, and I decide to break the ice for them. "Iris, why don't you tell Sam about school."

My daughter spends the next few minutes telling her dad about her teacher and her favorite subject. The more Iris talks the more she starts to relax, which makes us both relax more.

"Do you get good grades?" Sam asks.

Iris nods. "I do, don't I, Mommy."

"You do, baby." I smile at her and then turn to Sam. "She's very smart and so sweet." The waiter interrupts us and sets our food down in front of us. I snicker to myself at the way he looks at his food.

Iris is oblivious and digs into pad Thai with tofu and vegetables. I do the same with my eggplant.

Sam sets his fork down and turns to Iris. "Did you know you have a half-brother? His name is Nixon, and he's three. Your half-sister is going to be born any day now."

Iris looks at me and then back at him. "I have a brother." She claps excitedly. The rest of the lunch Iris asks question after question about her brother.

Sam's friendly, call it mother's intuition, but I don't buy it one hundred percent. Maybe I'm just protective, but I'm going to be very careful about all of this. I go to pay for our food when Sam waves us off and takes care of it.

Before we get up, I remind Iris to open the little gift bag. "Tawney picked it out," he says as our daughter pulls the tissue paper out.

"Iris, what is it, sweetheart?" She smiles and hands it to me.

I keep my face impassive when I see that it's a picture of Sam and his little family in a silver frame. He could've bought her a toy or some art supplies. Oh well, I should be grateful he got her anything at all. God, I sound like a snob or something.

"That's a great picture, Sam. Your son is adorable." The boy has light brown hair and eyes just like his dad.

"He's a handful, but thank you." Out on the sidewalk, he stops me with a hand on my arm. I really hate when he touches me. It may seem innocent, but it doesn't feel that way to me. "I'll call you about the party next week." He looks at Iris. "She'll need a party dress. You've got another check coming any day now, so you'll be able to afford it."

I bite my lip to keep from telling him that I could afford one without his money. I nod and grab Iris' hand. "Sounds good. Thank you for lunch."

Sam nods and then looks at Iris. "Goodbye. Can I maybe call you this week?"

Iris nods. "Sure!"

We walk hand in hand to the car, and I open the

back door for her. She climbs in and buckles her belt, and I do the same.

On the way to Joaquin's, I break the silence. "What did you think of Sam?"

In the rearview mirror, I watch her shrug. "He's okay." She glances out the window lost in thought, but then she asks a question I'm not prepared to answer. "Why didn't he want me until now?"

I turn the radio off. I can't avoid the question like I did the day before. "I think maybe he just wasn't ready for all the love you had to give." I'm pulling this out of my ass. "Sometimes grownups make decisions that they think are the right ones for them, but then it turns out that they're not. Give him a chance, okay?"

"I will; I promise." She looks around, taking in her surroundings. "Where are we going?"

"Well, Joaquin invited us over. Victoria made a bunch of desserts, and she needs help tasting them, so that's what we're going to do."

She shrieks so loud I'm surprised that the windows don't shatter immediately. "Oh, that makes me so happy." If Iris wasn't such an amazing artist, I'd tell her to go into acting with that performance.

I sing along to the radio, but when we hit the Buckhead District I'm suddenly reminded how little Joaquin and I have in common. He's money and power, and I'm tattoos, meditation, and colored hair. I'm very aware that it's a skewed way of thinking. I just haven't dated in so long, and Sam destroyed me.

Good thing we decided on friends with benefits.

We'll have fun, our kids will spend time together, and I'll keep my heart locked up tight.

We pull into the driveway and come to a stop next to his Range Rover. The front door opens, and Max and Fluffy come running out to us. Max, of course, bypasses me and runs right to Iris. Hand in hand they run toward the house. "Hi, Mona," he calls out behind him.

"Hey, Maximum." I squat, picking up Fluffy. "Hello, Fluffy." I kiss the top of his head, and his tongue immediately sneaks out and tags my neck. At the opening to the house, I find Joaquin leaning against the doorjamb.

God, he's too sexy for his own good. His t-shirt molds to his chest, and his jeans mold to his lean, muscular thighs. "Stop looking at me like that."

I smile up at him. "Stop looking so hot, and I won't ogle you."

"Ogle?" He laughs. I love the deep, rich tone of his laugh, and I swear my nipples are tingling.

He surprises me when he leans down, kissing my cheek. Did the temperature just go up because I'm suddenly very, very hot?

I set Fluffy down, and when I stand, my back comes in contact with a firm chest I'm very familiar with. His lips touch my ear. "Mmmm ... I love when you get all flushed."

Annddd ... now I'm wet. I turn around and give him my best mom face. "You better knock it off."

I hustle away from him and find his cousin in the kitchen talking to the kids. "Hey, Mona. Oh wow, I love that dress." She comes toward me and kisses both of my cheeks. "Iris was just telling us about lunch with her dad."

She leads me to a stool at the island and hands me a glass of white wine. How did she know this was what I needed? I drain half of the glass, and I don't miss that Joaquin is watching me.

"Come with me. Kids, we'll be right back, and don't eat all of the dessert."

With my hand in his firm grip, he drags/leads me to his office and shuts the door behind us. "How'd it really go?" He leans against his desk with his legs crossed at the ankles and his arms over his chest.

"It was honestly better than I expected, but I'm very leery of this. I'm trying not to be because I really do want her to have a relationship with him, but I don't trust him. He made partner at his firm, and they're having a party. Sam wants Iris there, and I'm scared to let her go without me. What if she needs me?" I hate that my history with her dad is making me extremely cautious.

JOAQUIN

I push off the desk and walk toward Mona. I pull her into my arms and hug her tight—ignoring the fact that we fit so well together and how great she feels in my arms. "Get her a phone. You can buy her one of those cheap little flip phones that she can keep on her with your number programmed in so she can call you."

She pulls back and smiles. "That's a great idea. Sorry I freaked a little bit there, but I'm protective of my baby."

I cup her cheek because I can't stop myself from touching her. "You didn't freak out, and it's great that Iris has a mom who has got her back. No matter what happens with him, she's got you. When she goes with him, just make sure you're very clear about the rules. I've had to remind Max's mom of the rules several times. He's my son. I have primary custody, so she has to follow the rules I set."

Mona nods. "Rules—got it. How did you handle it when Max would first go with your ex?"

"I'd do anything to keep my mind off of my boy being gone. I won't lie—
at first it was women, lots of women, but then the visits started to become further and further apart. He'd be moody when he came home, so I basically started sitting at home and watching the clock. Now I bury myself in my work." I step back. "You've got this."

"Thanks for talking to me and making me feel better." She wraps her arms around my waist and gives me a squeeze. "Now feed me some dessert."

I follow behind her, adjusting my thickening dick as my eyes zero in on her gorgeous ass. The kids both have chocolate covered lips.

"Here, you two, sit." Victoria sets two slices of chocolate cake in front of us. "This is a chocolate cake made with mayonnaise and a dark chocolate ganache in between each layer. The icing is chocolate buttercream.

Mona moans around a huge bite. I want to lick the frosting from her lips, but I turn back to mine and take my own bite. I moan as the chocolate flavor explodes on my tongue.

"Victoria, this is heaven in my mouth," Mona says. "The cake is so moist. You'd never know there was mayonnaise in it."

"Yay! I'm so glad you're liking it. Next I have a strawberry sorbet, and Max helped me puree the strawberries."

She sets little bowls in front of each of us.

Three desserts later and the kids are lying on the family room floor watching a movie, and Mona and I are cleaning up the kitchen while drinking coffee.

"I've never eaten so many desserts in my life, but I regret nothing," Mona says with a smile.

"Agreed, and I'm not normally a sweets person, but my cousin's got a gift. Do you guys have anything planned this coming week?" In just a short time, I've become addicted to her. I know I should pull back because we're dancing a fine line between friends with benefits and a full-blown relationship, but no one ever said I was smart.

Mona shakes her head as she picks up her coffee cup. "No, I don't think so. What's up?"

"Do you think you'd want to go have dinner?"

She moves around the counter and stops in front of me. "Does it make me sound bad if I ask if it can just be you and me? I'd love some adult only time." Mona covers her face. "I must sound like a horrible mother."

I grab her wrists and pull her hands down. "You don't sound like a horrible mother." I lean in until our lips are almost touching. Her sweet breath hits my lips. "I wouldn't mind a night alone with you."

"Great, I'll arrange a sitter. Either one of my sisters or my brother will watch them."

I smile because I can think of a ton of stuff she and I can do alone—preferably naked. Now my dick's hard thinking about getting her alone. I kiss her lips and then step back when I hear the kids chattering as they get close.

Iris goes right to her mom, wrapping her arms around her. "Is your movie done?" I ask my son who stops in front of me.

Max tips his head back and looks up at me. "Yeah. I'm hungry, what's for dinner?"

"How about I make you and Iris my world famous grilled cheese."

"That sounds good, Dad." My boy loves those and honestly would eat them every day if he could.

"Iris, how about my world famous grilled cheese?"

The little blonde smiles at me. "Sure, but my Mom makes the best."

I bark out a laugh. "She does, does she? Mona, how about a cook-off? We'll each make two then, the kids will taste them, and vote."

My lavender-haired beauty gives me a cocky grin. "You're going down."

"Yes, Roger, that sounds good. I'll have my assistant email you that list." I hang up, and my intercom beeps. "Yes, Lauren."

"Can I come in, dickhead." Lauren scolds Nick for his language. "Sorry, beautiful."

My door opens, and my best friend comes walking through. She laughs as she shuts the door. "You're something else. What brings you by?" I come around my desk, and we exchange a bro hug.

"Not much. I brought the contract if you could send it to your dad to look over." He hands me a manila envelope. "It's a pretty sweet deal. If your dad thinks it's on the up and up, then I'll sign. It'll be at least two years before I start making a profit, but when I do it'll be nice."

I pour us both a drink and hand him his tumbler filled with amber liquid. "I'll have my courier get them to him as soon as possible."

"That's great, man, I appreciate his time. Tell me, what's up with you and Mona?"

I lean back in my chair. "There's nothing to tell. We're friends; our kids are friends."

He looks at me like he's not buying it. "Just friends? Oh come on, you like her. Sierra said that any time they bring you up to Mona, she gets all starry-eyed."

Why does that make me feel good? Maybe because I *do* like her, and spending time with her and Iris makes me and my boy happy. I can't help but wonder if I should pull back and put us firmly in the friend zone, but I don't think I could do that.

"What's up with you and Sierra?" I know he has no problem sharing, or oversharing.

He claps his hands together. "Oh boy, she is fucking amazing. I've met my match with her. She knows how to wear a man out." Nick leans in. "She's very, very flexible."

I can only shake my head; although, she's stuck around longer than any other woman in Nick's life. "Just don't hurt her. That's Mona's sister, and I don't need shit getting awkward."

"Me hurt her? Ha, that's funny. She's the one who keeps breaking things off, but then is the one calling me to come over. I'm beginning to think I'm just her booty call."

I want to laugh because it sounds like karma is coming for Nick. I'm kind of interested to watch this play out.

I'm finished for the day, and I walk out with him. We make plans to meet for lunch later this week. He leaves me by my Rover. "You should tell her you like her and that you want her to be your girlfriend." Nick says the last in a singsong voice that makes me want to punch him in the balls.

"Get out of here, you moron." His deep laugh echoes through the garage as he walks to his Ford GT, one of the finest pieces of machinery that I've ever laid eyes on.

On my way home my phone rings. "What's up, prima?"

"Um … Melina is here. She wants to take Max for the night." Well, that took my good day and turned it into a bad one. She's not supposed to just show up.

"Fuck, okay; I should be home in about fifteen minutes. How's Max?"

"He seems to be doing okay. He's definitely surprised she's here, but I don't think he wants to go."

"Okay, I'm hanging up, but I'm hurrying."

In my driveway I find Melina's Mercedes sitting in my spot, but I don't care; I just want her gone. I take a deep breath before climbing out and making my way inside. Fluffy barks and comes running toward me. I scoop him up in my arms and walk further into the house.

I find my ex-wife standing next to the kitchen island where her new husband, Blaine, sits, showing Max something on his phone. The guy is okay, but he married Melina so I can't really trust his judgment; well, okay, that's not fair because I was married to her too.

"Joaquin," the bitch says as a way of greeting.

"Melina." I move to Max and ruffle his hair. "How was school?"

His smile that is so much like mine graces his lips. "It was good. Blaine's showing me pictures of their honeymoon. They went to the beach."

Blaine stands up and offers me his hand, and I take it. "How's it going, Joaquin?"

"Good, thanks. Congratulations on the wedding." A wedding my son was not invited to, I might add.

"Thank you."

I look at Max. "Hey, bud, why don't you go to your room for a few minutes while we talk, and we'll call you when we're done."

He slides off the stool and disappears. I turn to Melina. "You know you're not supposed to just show up. *We* don't like surprises."

"Oh, come on. What's wrong with me wanting to see my son?"

I can't believe her and the dipshit she married. That was one thing we agreed on; she was to call first and only come if I gave her permission. My son gets anxious when she's around … usually. Today's the first time Max has seemed okay, but that's probably because of Blaine.

"There are rules. I guarantee that if you had them and I chose not to follow them, you'd throw a tantrum. Now tell me why you're here?"

She comes around the counter to stand next to her husband. "We wanted to take Max to dinner and take him to our new place and show him his room there."

"He's got school tomorrow." Fuck, this sucks.

Blaine stands up. "We'll have him home by nine,

if that's okay with you."

As much as I'd like to deny her, I can't do that to Max. "Yeah, that's fine." I turn my head and shout, "Max, come down here."

A minute later I hear my son's footsteps as he comes running down the stairs and into the kitchen. "What, Dad?"

"Your mom and Blaine want to take you to dinner and then to their new house so you can see your room. Does that sound good?" He nods, so I tell him to go put on his shoes.

I walk them out and stand on the sidewalk, watching as they turn the car around and drive down the driveway. Once their car disappears from sight, I head inside and find Victoria coming toward me with her purse in her hand. "Where arc you off to?"

"Meeting some friends for drinks; do you want to come?"

I kiss her forehead. "Thank you for asking, but I'm going to pass."

She takes off, and I'm alone—well, me and Fluffy. I walk through the downstairs and realize just how quiet my home is without my son here. Fuck, I miss him already. I make a snap decision and grab my keys, wallet, and phone. Outside I hop into my Rover and make my way toward two of my favorite girls.

I pull up in front of their home and hop out, wondering if I should've called first.

I'm not sure how Mona is going to feel about me just showing up. A second later she's standing in the doorway smiling. "Hey! What are you doing here?" She pushes the screen door open, and I step inside.

"Sorry to just drop by, but Max's mom and new stepdad stopped by. Unexpectedly, I should mention as well, and they wanted to take him to dinner and to see his room at their new house. I wanted to say no, but I know that's not fair to him if she truly wants to be a mom." I scrub my hand through my hair and look her in the eye. "I'm a mess, sorry."

Mona wraps her arms around my waist. "You're not a mess. Was Max happy to go with them?"

"I wouldn't say happy, but he wasn't upset. I'm just pissed because she knows the rules. Melina knows not to just show up..."

"Joaq!" My favorite little blonde comes running into the living room and surprises me when she launches herself at me. I catch her in my arms, give her a hug, and set her down on the ground. "What are you doing here? Is Max here too?"

"Hi, gorgeous. Max is with his mom right now, so I thought I'd see what you ladies were up to."

"Mom's making veggie quesadillas." She butchers quesadilla, and it's adorable. "Do you want to stay for dinner? Mom, can he?"

Mona smiles at her daughter and then looks to me. "Do you want to stay?"

"I'd like that."

Iris disappears down the hall, and I follow Mona into the kitchen. "I'm not intruding, am I? I can go."

"You're not intruding. Do you want a beer? I think I have Sam Adams." My eyes go to her ass as she sticks her head in the refrigerator. She grabs a bottle, and when she stands up, she catches me looking. "You're bad."

I take the beer and shrug. "I can't help it." I lean

in. "You've got a great ass."

She pushes up on her toes and presses her lips to mine. "Thanks, I know." She turns with an exaggerated sway of her hips. Mona opens the oven and pulls out what looks like a pizza stone. That's when an incredible smell hits me and makes my stomach growl.

"That smells incredible."

"Thanks. These are Iris' favorite." I watch mesmerized as she cuts the huge veggie filled tortilla into slices. She grabs a bowl out of the refrigerator and sets it on the table.

"Do you need help?"

She smiles and shakes her head before calling for Iris who comes running out. "I'm starving," she says dramatically as she pulls out her chair. "Come sit by me, Joaq."

I pull out the chair next to her and sit. Once Mona joins us, I help Iris put a couple slices on her plate as well as salad. We're all silent as we dig in, and to be honest this is really fucking good.

They're cheesy, spicy, and a lot more filling than I thought they'd be. I grab my napkin and wipe my mouth. "How's school, Iris? Are you learning lots?"

"I love school. It would be better if Max was there with me, but I'm really good at math and art."

"That's great, sweetheart."

While Iris continues to eat, Mona and I talk about the studio. "Right now we're booking two months out. I have a couple more openings, and then I'm going to have to close my books. We're thinking about taking on an apprentice, but it's hard to trust someone with your business. I mean, if they

120

screw up, it's on us. Then again, my old boss gave me a chance, and I should do it for someone else."

"How does that work? Do they apply?" I take a drink of my beer.

Mona shakes her head. "Well, kind of. Usually, if someone wants to apprentice with us, they'll bring their artwork in, and we'll look it over. If we think they have the skillset to work with our team, then we go over apprenticing responsibilities and duties."

She takes a drink of whatever is in her purple glass. "I've always hated telling them no, but it just hasn't been the right time. I'll talk to my sisters and see what they say."

After we finish eating, I send Mona into the living room to relax. "Iris, why don't you help me clean up the kitchen."

"Okay, Joaq," she chirps and happily skips to the sink with dirty plates in her hands.

I rinse them off and stick them in the dishwasher. Iris hands me the dirty silverware. "Thank you, *preciosita*."

She smiles up at me and takes the washcloth and wipes down the table. I start the dishwasher and take the washcloth from Iris, rinse it off, and lay it on the edge of the sink.

I find Mona curled up in the corner of the sofa with a cat in her lap while she reads her e-reader.

She looks up as I sit next to her. "Thanks for cleaning up the kitchen. Thank you for helping, Iris." The little blonde flops down on the other side of me. I wrap my arm around her little shoulders and hug her to my side.

I feel Mona's eyes on me, and when I look at her, she's smiling, and her eyes are shining. Almost as fast, her face goes blank, and she looks away. I grab her hand, pulling her to me and wrapping my other arm around her.

I lean back, propping my ankle on my knee, and hug both of my girls—*my girls?* Who am I kidding? I'm falling for the lavender-haired beauty and her beautiful daughter. I'm not ready for this; it's too soon. I don't have time for a relationship ... right?

I should get up right now and walk out the door, but I don't. Instead, I listen as Iris tells me all about her teacher with the same exuberance that Max does. Fuck, I wish he was here.

"Ms. Michaels told Hunter that he can't tease the girls, but I don't let him tease me. He tried, but I told him I'd kick his balls."

I choke out a laugh, but quickly cover it with a cough. "How do you know about kicking boys in the balls?"

Iris looks at me seriously. "Aunt Greta told me. She said boys who are mean deserve it."

I look at Mona, and she just shakes her head. "Iris, what did I tell you about repeating grown-up stuff that your aunts and uncle say to you?"

"You said not to," she says with a huff. "Joaq, do you want me to draw you something?"

"That'd be great, sweetheart. Draw me whatever you want." Iris disappears down the hall leaving Mona and me alone. I grab her chin, tilting her head back. "I just need to feel your lips."

She leans in, and our lips touch as soft as a whisper. Our tongues brush, and a soft moan slips from her lips. All too soon the kiss ends.

We snuggle on the sofa for a little while longer before I need to go. "I should be going; Max will be home soon." I stand and pull Mona to her feet and wrap my arms around her. "When can I see you again?"

"I could come over tomorrow after I take Iris to school."

My dick twitches in my pants thinking about burying myself inside her in the morning. "That sounds perfect." We're interrupted before I can kiss her again, when Iris comes out holding a sheet of paper. "Let's see it, *preciosita.*"

Iris hands it to me, and I look down. It's a beautiful butterfly with a unicorn horn sticking out of the top. At the bottom it says *from Iris,* and she puts a little heart above the second I. This girl has stolen my heart, and she doesn't even know it.

I wrap my arm around her and hug her to my side. "This is beautiful. Thank you so much."

She beams with pride as she looks up at me. "You can hang it up in your office so you can see it every day."

"That's a great idea, and I have the perfect place for it." I look at Mona. "I really should go. Walk me out?"

"Iris, I'll be right back."

The little blonde hugs me and then disappears down the hall. Mona steps outside with me and walks me to my Rover. "I'll see you in the morning?"

"Yeah. Oh, don't let me forget to tell you about our lunch with Sam. It went pretty good." She looks relieved about that.

I bend down and kiss her cheek. "That's great, *Corazoncita.* See you in the morning." She waves as I pull away.

 ELEVEN

MONA

Joaquin moans as I swirl my tongue around the head of his cock. Pre-cum coats my tongue as I suck him deep into my mouth. Fuck, he's so big and tastes good. When I got here I was wearing a little sundress that he basically ripped off of me the moment I stepped inside, and he shut the door.

No words were spoken—we didn't need them. The sexual tension was so high between us that I swear I almost came the moment he kissed me. He carried me to his bedroom and tossed me on his bed, which brings us to now.

He's on his back with his knees bent, and I'm kneeling between them. My hand is wrapped around the thick base, and my mouth engulfing him. Joaquin's fingers spear my hair, and he grips it tight and controls the motion.

"Fuck, baby, your mouth is so fucking hot and so fucking wet," he groans, his voice laced with desire. "Shit, no more; I need to fuck you."

I'm up, and the next thing I know he's sheathing

125

his cock, rolling us, and sliding between my thighs. He leans down until his lips are brushing mine. "Are you ready for me to fuck you?" I nod. "Is my girl going to moan when I slide inside her?" I whimper.

I feel the head of Joaquin's cock as he nudges my opening. He pulls back and holds my eyes as he slides into me to the hilt.

Something deep—something important—passes between us, and then his lips are on mine. Things become frenzied between us. He gives two hard thrusts before flipping us so he's on his back, and I'm riding him.

Joaquin sits up and sucks on my nipples until I come hard, crying out his name over and over. "Fuck, you just got really hot and really wet." He gets on his knees, taking me with him. I wrap my legs around his hips and grab on to his biceps.

I'm going to have bruises from where he's gripping my hips, but I don't care—I relish the bite of pain. Joaquin bounces me up and down on his cock, and our position causes him to be so deep inside me, causing me to cry out with each thrust.

I'm not petite by any means, but he's picking me up and moving me around like I weigh nothing. I grab his face, tilting it up and kissing him hard. Our tongues duel, his grip becomes punishing, and I moan into his mouth as I come again.

Joaquin pulls me down once, twice, and then I feel him jerk inside me as he begins to come.

We both pant, and then I'm falling back with him following, but catching himself on his forearm. He kisses my forehead, the tip of my nose, and then my lips. The brush of his lips is so tender that it warms me deep inside and makes me fall even harder for him.

I knew it would happen; I knew the friends with benefits would be a bad idea. I knew that I could possibly fall hard for this man, and that's what I've done. The first time I felt it was lying in this bed, and he talked to me about Iris' spelling test; something so simple meant so much.

Last night when he wrapped his arm around Iris' shoulders and then mine, hugging us both to his sides, that was the icing on the cake.

"Mona?"

I focus back on Joaquin. "Sorry, I think you broke my brain." I laugh and bury my face in his neck, hoping he can't see my feelings that are probably written all over my face.

He pulls out, and I whimper at the loss of him inside me. "I'll be right back." He walks naked into the master bathroom, and I hug his pillow to my chest. The woodsy, manly scent that is all him surrounds me.

I hear the toilet flush and the sink turn on and off before Joaquin steps into his bedroom in all his naked glory. He's got the body of an athlete and the cock of a porn star. Even mostly soft, his dick is impressive.

"Don't stare at me like that, dirty girl. I've got a meeting at eleven." He crawls onto the bed and pulls his pillow away from me before climbing between my thighs and smiling down at me. "I could stay here all day."

I reach up, brushing his hair back. I love seeing it like this, messy and free of product. It's so soft under my fingers, and there's a natural wave to it. "Me too."

He's quiet for a minute, and then something changes—he looks troubled ... conflicted. His brow is furrowed, his lips are pinched tight, and the muscle in his jaw ticks. "I think ... I think it's time we end this. Neither of us wants a relationship, and that's exactly what's starting to happen. I don't want to hurt you, and I've loved every second we've spent together."

"What?" I whisper. A knot forms in my throat, and my eyes begin to burn—maybe he's right, but that doesn't make this hurt any less. I push the pain back and let myself get fucking pissed. This whole thing was his idea; he wanted this. I let my daughter care about him, and he let me care about Max.

He was just inside of me, and now he's ending it, just like that? I push at his shoulders. "Get off me."

"Please don't be like this, Mona. I didn't mean for this to happen." I ignore him and quickly run out into the foyer where my dress is and throw it on. I ignore Joaquin as he continues to call my name.

I manage to make it outside to my car and drive out of the driveway before he comes running outside in shorts. The burning in my eyes just pisses me off further.

Once I get home, I immediately jump in the shower, scrubbing *him* from my body. Tears leak from my eyes because, again, I was stupid and let myself fall for someone who was so far out of my league.

After I climb out of the shower, I moisturize and then throw on my robe before letting my hair down.

I hit it with the hairdryer, drying the end pieces that got wet, and try to forget about him.

I try not to think about Joaquin as I put makeup on. I throw on a worn pair of jean capris and my Lady Gaga concert shirt from when my sisters and I took Iris when she was five.

Peanut comes walking out of Iris' room. "Are you hungry, boy?"

He looks at me and gives me a meow.

I follow him into the kitchen and fill his bowl. While he eats, I brew a cup of coffee and pop a piece of bread into the toaster. When that's done, I slather it in apple butter and only eat half before I toss the rest out. It didn't taste good anyway.

I can't be here right now—the quiet is making my thoughts too loud. It's better to keep myself busy, so I don't think about him or the pain in my chest.

After wiping the tattoo off that I just finished, I let him go take a look at it in the mirror. I clean off my station while Greta takes a picture of his tattoo for our website and social media sites. She covers it for me and gives him the aftercare instructions.

When Greta's done, I take him to the counter. We worked for about five hours, and that's about eight hundred dollars. He tips me and tells me not to be surprised that he's going to be coming back.

I wipe off my chair, and when I look up, my sisters are all staring at me. "What?"

"Why do you look sad? What's wrong?" Sierra

knows me too well, but I honestly don't want to talk about it right now. I'm embarrassed that I let myself fall for someone who just wanted sex from me.

"I'm just tired, and I woke up with a headache."

Sierra sighs. "Fine, if that's the story that you're sticking to. I do have something that I want to talk to you about." She looks between me and our other two sisters. We're all not usually here at the same time, but today we are.

"What's up?" I sit on my stool and give her my undivided attention.

"There's an Ink'd expo coming next spring, and they want us to be their featured artists. We'll do some tattoos, and then they want to do a Q&A with us about our studio. This could be great exposure for us. What do you think?"

We've had booths at other conventions or expos before. We don't make a ton of money, but we definitely get lots of attention. It's not hard to know why ... because we're all attractive women. It is kind of irritating but once they see what we can do, what we look like no longer matters.

"I think it's great, and anything to bring more attention to our studio the better. This is probably also a good time to bring up that I think we should take on an apprentice. I'm ready to mentor someone." I grab my water and take a drink.

"That might be cool," Heidi says with a smile. "We can always use the extra help." She looks at me closely. "Are you sure you're okay?"

"I promise I'm fine. I'm done for the day, so maybe I'll go home and lay down before Miles brings Iris back."

"Why doesn't Iris spend the night with Greta and me?" Heidi and Greta are roommates. "I can take her to school in the morning." Greta steps in close. "Take the night to pamper yourself; take a bath, drink some wine, read a book, or meditate. Even better, go have some sex with that sexy man of yours."

My stomach turns, and I try hard to keep my voice neutral. "Yeah, I don't think so. I'm just going to head home. I'll call Miles and tell him the plan."

I kiss my sisters and take my leave. When I get home, I've let Miles know that Greta will be picking up Iris. My daughter and I talk for a few minutes, and I promise to call her before bed.

I grab the mail before letting myself inside. Peanut greets me at the door with a meow and winds around my legs.

"Hi, pretty boy." I reach down, scratching him behind his ear. He follows me into the kitchen, where I toss the mail. I grab my bottle of chardonnay and a wine glass. While I take a generous sip, I flip through the mail. The bottom envelope draws my attention.

I set my glass down and open the envelope to see that it's another check for one thousand dollars. I close my eyes and take a deep breath. Sam's actually following through with what he said.

I leave it on the counter and carry my wine into my bedroom and set it on the nightstand. I lie down on my side and close my eyes thinking about this morning. I still can't figure out what caused the change in Joaquin.

I wasn't looking for a relationship either, and I

certainly wasn't expecting to fall for him, but I did. Maybe he saw that and that's why he did end it. He must not have felt the same way about me. I roll to my back and stare at the ceiling. What am I going to do about Max and Iris? They're best friends, and it would kill them if they couldn't see each other.

I'm not going to wallow in any of it right now. I sit up and drain my glass of wine. I carry it into the kitchen and decide to try some meditation to clear my mind. I light some amber-scented incense, and the smell fills up my living room as I pull my pillow out and then sit down.

"Alexa, play my meditation mix." The soft piano starts to play, and I get situated and rest my palms on my thighs.

In and out I breathe, letting my mind go blank.

An unknown amount of time passes before my eyes pop open. Peanut lays on the floor in front of me, watching me no doubt. I feel tired and heavy and decide to take a nap—something I rarely get to do. In no time my eyes drift shut.

"Why can't I talk to Max? You know he's my best friend." Iris puts her hands on her hips.

I knew it was only a matter of time before she asked about him. It's only been twenty-four hours since Joaquin basically ended things, and I've been doing everything I can to distract myself.

Last night after my nap, I cleaned the bathroom and the kitchen. I called Iris, who was being spoiled by her aunts, and told her goodnight. She was yawning as we spoke, and I knew my girl would be asleep in no time. I promised her before hanging up that tonight we'd have homemade pizza.

Sleep didn't claim me until well past one in the morning, but my thoughts were consumed by Joaquin and Sam—two men that I let into my life that I shouldn't have.

Of course, I shouldn't compare the two because Joaquin wouldn't have walked out on me the way Sam did. Logically, I know I have no reason to be mad at Joaquin because we both agreed to the terms of our arrangement, and he was just doing the right thing. If he did the right thing, then why do I feel so sad? Again, it's because I was stupid and fell for the man.

"You just can't, Iris. Now stop asking." Her chin wobbles, and I take a deep breath. I didn't mean to snap at her, but she's been bugging me about it since we got home. "I'm sorry." I wrap my arms around her. "Come, let's make pizza."

I've just thrown our pizzas in the oven when my phone rings. I rush toward it—part of me hoping that it's Joaquin, but when I see it's Sam, my stomach sinks and disappointment fills me.

Two days ago we did another lunch, and Sam brought his son. It went better than the first meeting, and Nixon being there helped make things more relaxed. The little boy sat by me and traced the tattoos on my arm closest to him while Iris and Sam talked.

My daughter was definitely more at ease which made me feel a lot better about things, even though I still don't want to share her.

133

The ringing pulls my attention back to my cell phone. "Hey, Sam."

"Hey, Mona, how are you? Did you get the check?"

"I'm good, and I did; thanks." Ugh. He needs to just get on with what he wants. "What's up?"

Sam clears his throat. "I was wondering if I could talk to Iris for a few minutes. You know, see how she's doing."

"Yeah, let me get her for you." I pull the phone from my ear and move down the hall. Iris is sitting at her little desk drawing. "Baby, your dad is on the phone and wants to talk to you." God, that sounds weird to say.

My heart does warm when Iris smiles widely before taking the phone from me. "Hi, Sam, how are you? Is my brother good?"

I smile at her excitement as she listens to whatever he says. She keeps listening and her face changes slightly, maybe not enough for someone who doesn't know her to notice, but Iris' excitement wanes. "Okay, here's Mom." Iris pauses. "Bye."

She hands the phone back to me. "What's up, Sam?"

"That party I was telling you about is this coming weekend. I'd like for Iris to be there. We'll come get her and bring her home after, if that works for you?"

I pinch the bridge of my nose. "Um … yeah I think that would be okay, but I'll come get her when the party is over. There's no sense in you driving her all the way home afterward."

"Okay, yeah, that would be great. Tawney would

prefer that Iris wears a dress that's either a light yellow or mint green and white shoes."

Ugh, of course, he wants to dictate what my daughter wears. "Anything else?" I can't keep the sarcasm out of my voice.

"Mona, it's not a big deal. We just want her to coordinate with us." I'm sure the wife is the one who instigated that, but then Sam always wanted things just so.

"I'll get her a dress that'll go with your color scheme. What time are you picking her up?"

I hear him ask someone something in the background. "I'll be there to get her around one."

We hang up, and I turn toward Iris who followed me into my bedroom and sat next to me on the bed. "How do you feel about going with your dad?"

She shrugs "I won't know anyone."

"Yeah, but you'll get to know your brother more and Sam's wife. I bet you'll have a great time. Tomorrow, we're going dress shopping and finding you the prettiest dress." I wrap my arms around her. "I'm going to buy you your own phone. I want you to keep it on you at the party. If at any time you want me to come get you, you just call me. Just give it a chance. You might have a great time."

"Okay, Mom." Iris hugs me tight, and I send up vibes that my daughter has an amazing time.

JOAQUIN

"I needed those contracts yesterday. If they're not on my desk by tomorrow morning, I'll be looking for a new lawyer." I slam my phone down and push my chair away from my desk.

I know I'm being a dick, I do, and it's my fault. The moment Mona left earlier this week, I knew I'd made a huge mistake, and guilt filled me. I've been miserable ever since, and I have been taking it out on everyone around me, even Max, which I hate.

Max has been asking every day to talk to Iris, but I've told him no. I'm not sure that Mona would even accept my call or hasn't already blocked me. Okay, let's be honest—I haven't called because I'm a chicken shit.

I'll admit I broke things off because she scares me; what I feel for her and her daughter scares me. Melina did a bang-up job screwing with my head, and then watching her bebop in and out of Max's life without caring or knowing him really did a number on me. Fuck with me, fine, but fuck with my son—well, that's another story.

I know Mona's nothing like my ex-wife; she's loving, compassionate, funny, sexy and a fucking amazing mother. Hell, she's shown my son more love and care than his own mother.

Fuck, I can't stop thinking about her or the look on her face when I ended things.

I stand and walk to the window. The view of the skyline still takes my breath away. Yes, I was born into money and have never struggled a day in my life, but I've worked my ass off for everything I have. I may have worked for my father, and once he retired he and his partners voted me in, and I kept his clients, turning this business into what it is today.

I step out of my office and stop at Lauren's desk. "Can you send Roger a box of those cigars he likes and a bottle of Macallan."

"Of course. I'll have them sent over immediately." She smiles up at me.

"Thank you." I head back into my office.

I work for a couple hours until Victoria comes walking into my office. "What are you doing here?" I stand and come around my desk, kissing her cheek.

"Have you called her?" I shake my head. "Why not? You said it yourself that you made a mistake." The day I ended it with Mona, I drowned my sorrows in beer after Max went to bed and told Victoria what happened.

"I don't know what to say."

"Tell her you're sorry. For the love of God, just

do it because you've been such a grump all week long." She grabs my hand. "If you're not feeling her that's fine, but your kids are best friends and Max misses Iris."

"I'm falling hard for Mona. I'm falling hard for her daughter. It scares the fuck out of me."

Victoria grabs my shoulders. "Don't you think that you and Max deserve to be happy? Even if a relationship doesn't happen between the two of you, you guys can work on building a friendship so that your kids can continue being friends."

"You're right. I'll call her. Maybe take her out to dinner so we can talk."

"Good, now take me to lunch."

She loops her arm through mine, and I take my cousin to lunch.

I strip my t-shirt off and use it to wipe the sweat from my face. I loop it over the handle of the mower and continue moving across my yard. My father never understood why I didn't hire someone to maintain my yard, but I like doing it.

We do have a maid who comes twice a month to do a deep clean, but in between that, Victoria and I work together to keep the place clean.

I haven't called Mona yet—I've been thinking very hard about what to say to her. I don't want to screw it up. Shit, I'm not ever this self-conscious about anything. I need to lay it all out to her.

I focus on the lawn while the late summer sun beats down on me. Once I finish, I push the mower into the shed and grab the weed whacker. I love how big our backyard is, but I hate how long it fucking takes to take care of it.

Once I finish, I head inside and take a cold shower. I promised Max that we could go see a movie tonight. It's the least I can do since he's had to see me be a real prick this week.

After my shower, I throw on jeans, a t-shirt, and black Nikes and then head out to find my son. In the family room, I find him and Fluffy playing on the floor. "Hey, bud. Do you still want to go see a movie later?"

"Yeah, can we go see the new Lego movie?" I'm not a fan of them, but my boy is. I suppose I can suffer through an hour and half cartoon for him.

"I'll check the times, but yeah, we can go see it." Max gives a little fist pump from the floor. I pull the app up on my phone and see that we can go at six-thirty. "Okay, bud, I'm going to do a couple of things in my office before dinner and then we'll go see the movie.

I head into my office and sit behind my desk. I log into my computer and pull up the stocks I want to watch for a bit. While I wait for the information to come up, my eyes drift to the picture that Iris drew for me. As I stare at it I can't help but think that it would make a gorgeous tattoo.

I turn back to my computer and watch my monitors for a few minutes, making notes about the stocks I've been keeping an eye on. A couple clients have been asking about these, and before I buy shares I like to watch them for a while to see how they do.

Once I'm done, I reheat some taco meat that Victoria made the night before. Max and I sit at the island and eat some tacos. He's only seven, but he's a bottomless pit. I can't seem to make him full because I cut him off at three huge tacos. I can't imagine what it'll be like when he's a teenager.

My boy finishes up, and I send him to brush his teeth while I quickly load the dishwasher and get it running. I quickly let Fluffy out and then brush my own teeth. Max waits by the door to the garage, bouncing on the balls of his feet.

Thankfully I picked the theater that serves alcohol, so I order myself a beer and popcorn and soda for Max. We head to our theater and find spots in the second row. Max happily munches on his popcorn.

The lights go down as the previews start. I grab a handful of popcorn and munch on it as Max laughs from beside me for some new action movie that he can't wait to see I'm sure.

My phone vibrates in the little cup holder. I grab it and look, my heart racing when I see Mona's name pop up on the screen. I send her a message that we're in the movie, and I'll call her when we're done.

A message from her pops up, and the hairs on the back of my neck stand up.

Mona: Iris went to a party with her dad and his family today. My girl had a terrible time and is so sad. Can you bring Max over to see her? You don't have to talk to me, but please do this for her.

I lean into Max. "Hey, bud, Mona just texted me,

141

and Iris is having a really bad day. Should we go see her when we're done?"

My boy doesn't even have to think about it. "Can we go now?"

"Are you sure? We can go as soon as it's over."

He stands and makes his way toward the exit with me bringing up the rear. How did I get so lucky being this kid's dad?

We pull up in front of Mona and Iris' house. Max unbuckles his belt and climbs out of the back. He opens the front passenger door and grabs the box of cupcakes we picked up as well as the bouquet of pink roses Max wanted to get for her.

Mona opens the door as we approach. She smiles down at Max. "Hey, Maximum. How are you, buddy?" He wraps his full hands around her hips.

"I'm good." Max let's go and disappears inside.

I take in the beautiful woman standing in front of me. Mona's hair is in one of those messy knots, and she's got one of those wide headbands on. Her white tank top molds to her gorgeous breasts and shows off her tanned skin. All of her ink is on full display, and I ache to touch each tattoo with my tongue. The black shorts she's wearing show off her long, shapely legs.

"Hi," she says. I don't miss the unshed tears or her wobbling chin.

I step toward her—not stopping until I wrap my arms around her. "How bad was it?"

She doesn't speak at first, but she does wrap her arms around me. "No one would talk to her. Sam's little boy was being a monster, and they expected Iris to watch him. He threw food on the floor, and then Sam's wife said that Iris should've stopped him. The worst is that they had a photographer and when Iris went to stand next to them, Sam's asshole father made her get out of the picture. Sam didn't even try to stop him."

It's taking all I have not to hop in my Rover and go after that motherfucker. "I'm so sorry, sweetheart. She doesn't deserve that. What can I do?"

"Bringing Max is a good start."

I pull back enough to look down at her. "I'm sorry about what I had said. I didn't mean..."

She covers my mouth with her hand and shakes her head. "I don't want to talk about that right now."

Mona leads me inside, and I follow her down the hall. We stand in the doorway and watch as Max and Iris sit on the floor with the cupcakes and flowers. My boy talks quietly to the little girl who looks completely defeated.

I grab Mona's hand and pull her down the hall and into the kitchen. She's clearly holding on by a thread. Tears shimmer in her eyes, and again her chin begins to wobble. I pull her to me and whisper into her ear, "Let it out; I've got you."

Mona cries hard as I hold her in their little kitchen. I don't say anything; I just let her get it out. When her cries finally quiet, I pull back, cupping her face with my hands and brushing the tears away with my thumbs.

I lean in kissing her forehead. "She's a strong little girl. Iris will get through this."

She nods. "I know, but I'm so mad that she even had to deal with that. I took your advice and got her a phone. I told her to call me, and I'd come pick her up whenever." Mona takes a deep breath. "Iris was there for an hour and a half before she called. Sam was so pissed when I showed up. I was wearing this, and I didn't care."

"What happened?"

"Nothing, I found my daughter and then found Sam and told him that we were leaving. His dad, the pompous asshole, said some unflattering things that I don't care to repeat. I picked my daughter up and carried her out." She gets quiet. "Iris cried the whole way home."

She pulls herself together and takes a deep breath. I follow her down the hall back to the kids. "Hey, guys." Mona walks further into the room. "Iris, why don't you thank Joaquin for bringing Max over."

The little blonde who has stolen my heart hops up and wraps her arms around my waist, resting her cheek against my stomach. "Thank you, Joaq."

I wrap my arms around her. "Anything for you, *preciosita*. Why don't we take those cupcakes and flowers into the kitchen, and we can enjoy them together." She smiles up at me and nods.

The four of us sit around Mona's table eating cupcakes—the kids drink milk, while Mona and I drink coffee. Conversation is light and easy while we sit around the table together, but one thing I do know is that this all feels right.

I hope to God Mona will give me another chance, and I can make things right.

After the kids polish off their cupcakes, they go into Iris' room to watch a movie on Mona's laptop, giving us some time alone to talk. She flits around the kitchen, avoiding me, but that's okay. She'll have to sit down eventually.

I grab our coffee cups and carry them to the sink. Mona tries to move past me, but I stop her. "Can we please talk? There are some things I want to say to you. Will you let me do that?"

Mona stares at me for a moment and then finally nods. I let out a sigh of relief. I lead her to the table and have her take a seat. I sit next to her, sitting so we're facing each other, and I grab her hands. "I'm sorry that I got scared. Truth is, I've fallen for you, for that little girl in there, and it scared me."

I bring her hands to my lips and kiss them. "I know I said I didn't want a relationship, and I didn't—not until you. I want you to give us a shot; I want us to date."

"I don't know, Joaquin. The way you broke things off really hurt me. We'd had sex and were still naked when you ended it."

"I know, and I'm very aware of how much that was a mistake, but I can't predict the future, baby. I know that I want to spend time with you and Iris. This is scary, and there are four hearts involved, but shouldn't we at least try?" I hold her hands to my lips while she seems to be mulling it over.

I've never been more nervous. I know there's a lot at stake, but we owe it to ourselves to try.

"Please don't break my heart," Mona whispers.

"You know that neither of us can make that promise because you could just as easily break mine."

She gives me a hesitant smile and surprises me

when she whispers, "Kiss me."

I let go of her hands, grab her face, and pull her to me. "Fuck, you're bossy."

Mona leans in meeting me halfway. Her lips are a hairsbreadth away from mine, and she whispers against my lips, "You've got that right."

The kiss is soft, sweet, and not as deep I want to take it, but we're not alone. At any minute the kids could come out and catch us. Our tongues lightly touch, and I pull her closer, spreading my legs a little wider for her to fit in between.

I need to pull back, about to lose control.

"Ooooohhh…" Mona and I freeze. I turn my head to find Iris and Max standing in the opening of the kitchen. "Were you guys kissing?" Max asks, coming to stand next to me. I pull away from Mona so Iris can wrap her arms around her.

I open my mouth to speak, but Mona beats me to it. "We were. Does that upset you? Or you?" She looks from Max to Iris.

Max is the first to speak. "Nah …It's just gross."

"Oh, *mijo,* you won't think it's gross in a few years, and I seem to remember a certain little boy and girl who got caught kissing at school."

"Oh yeah, it's still gross." My son shakes his head, starts to laugh, and grabs Iris' hand. She lets go of her mom's waist and lets him lead her out of the room.

Mona's smiling and shaking her head. "Besides us kissing and it being gross, that went really well." She's quiet for a moment. "Are you sure this is what you want?"

"Yes, and I will prove it to you." The doorbell

rings, and Mona walks toward the front door.

I follow behind her and don't miss the way her body stiffens when she looks through the peephole. She looks at me. "It's Sam."

My jaw ticks as I clench it. Every fiber of my being is telling me to jump in and intervene, but I don't think Mona would appreciate that.

She takes a deep breath and pulls the door open. "What are you doing here, Sam?"

"What the fuck was that earlier, Mona? You embarrassed me showing up like that. My father is not happy with you." I can't see him, but my fists clench.

"Mommy, who's here?" Iris says as she comes into the living room with Max following close behind. She moves to stand by her mom. "What do you want?"

"Iris, you can't talk to me like that," Sam says, and I decide it's time for me to step in.

I pull the door open and put Mona and Iris behind me. "Can I help you, friend?"

"We're not friends, and this doesn't concern you."

I take a deep breath. "You're right, we're not friends, but you're wrong about it not concerning me because it does. I can see you're upset, but you're not going to just show up and lay into Mona. Why don't you go home and calm down, and Mona can call you tomorrow, and you can talk."

This guy is the typical rich boy, spoiled brat that becomes a spoiled adult—I've dealt with guys like him all my life. My parents may have made mistakes when I was growing up, but at least my father taught me the importance of hard work.

The douche seems to mull it over. "Fine." He turns and walks down the sidewalk to his SUV, hops in, and drives away.

I turn to Mona and the kids. "Kids, why don't you pick out a movie for all of us to watch? Mona and I are going to go talk real quick." I grab Mona's hand and pull her into her bedroom. "Are you okay?"

"Yes, thank you for handling that. I can't believe he had the nerve to show up here like that. Should I be worried?" She shifts from one foot to the other.

"No, if anything he's just going to be a huge pain in your ass."

Mona wraps her arms around her stomach. "When Sam and I dated, I thought he was so charming, but the first time his dad insulted me, Sam wouldn't stand up for me. His dad basically said I was out to trap him, and that when he was fucking me, he better be smart and wear a condom."

That makes my blood boil. The man is obviously a piece of shit if he can't see how amazing this woman truly is.

"I was so young and stupid. I should've broken up with him long before that, but then I can't regret it because I wouldn't have my daughter."

I pull her into a hug. "It'll be okay. I promise."

I hope I can keep that promise.

MONA

It's been two weeks since Joaquin and I became an us. We've spent time together when we can. Between both of our careers and our kids, we're both busy. We do talk every night before bed as do the kids.

Sam's called a few times to talk to Iris, but he hasn't attempted to see her again. My daughter is leery of him now, and I hate it. If she decides that she doesn't want to see him, then I'll abide by her wishes.

I focus on the laptop and pay the bills for the studio. When no one else is here, that's when I get the most work done. I love my sisters and couldn't do this without them, but they love to distract me when I'm trying to do the work that they voted for me to do.

Once I pay the last one, I file all of the bills with their confirmation numbers written on them into their folders. I hear the chime of the front door opening and know that whoever it is has a key.

A moment later Miles is standing in the doorway. "Hey. What are you doing here?" I come around my desk and wrap my arms around him.

"I hit my word count for the day and knew you'd be here paying bills. How about we go out to lunch?"

I grab my phone and check my schedule. "Sure. My first client isn't for a couple hours." After shutting down my laptop, I grab my purse and follow Miles out. He leads me to his Jeep Cherokee and opens the door for me.

On the way to our favorite sandwich shop, he tells me the plot of the next book he's going to be writing. Ever since he was little, he would make up these elaborate stories. Our parents really supported his craft. Hell, they've always supported us and our choices—even if they didn't understand the whole tattoo thing at first.

We reach Happy's and head inside, grabbing a table by the window. Our waitress takes our order and goes to get our drinks.

"How are things going with Joaquin?" He's the only one of my siblings who knows what happened when Joaquin broke things off. I needed to talk to someone, and my brother was the best bet.

"Good, except we haven't really had time together lately. Between the studio and Iris, I've been swamped. He's been really busy too."

Our waitress sets our drinks down in front of us. "If you want I can take Iris for the weekend, so you guys can spend some time together."

"You're sweet to offer. I'll talk to him and see what he wants to do. I know his cousin usually watches Max, but he tries not to do anything without his son during the weekends. He likes to give Victoria breaks." I love that about Joaquin. He doesn't just dump his kid off on other people so he can have a social life.

"If he's cool with it, I could take him too. From what you've said he sounds like a good kid."

My brother should be nominated for sainthood, always doing good deeds for others. "Okay. I'll talk to Joaquin and see what he says. You're too good to me."

I wish he'd let me set him up on dates. I know he's no virgin or anything, but he works all the time. Granted, he's doing what he loves, but I'd love for him to meet a wonderful girl who would treasure the gift that he is.

He pays for lunch, refusing to let me do it, and leads us outside. When he drops me off, I promise to let him know the game plan for the weekend.

Inside, the music's on, and the buzz of a tattoo machine fills the space. Jen is behind the counter on the phone. I give her a wave as I head to my station and get ready for my appointment.

Five hours later, I stand up and stretch my back. I push my glasses up on top of my head and peel my gloves off. "Go ahead and take a look at it in the mirror. Stretch your legs a bit, and then I want to get a picture of it."

Renee looks at the flowers on her arm. The tears that slide down her cheek make me smile because I know she loves it and what it means to her. Five years ago she lost her husband and daughter in a car accident. The flowers are those of their birth months as well as the month that they died.

Renee got married two years ago and has a son with her new husband, and he paid for this tattoo so she'd always remember them. I heard the whole story the day she came in to discuss her design, and I knew I wanted to create a beautiful memorial for her lost husband and daughter.

She comes over to me. "I love it so much." Her voice cracks. "This is just what I wanted."

I grab her hand. "I'm so glad. Thank you for trusting me to do it." I pick up my phone and open the camera app. "Let me get a quick picture, and then we'll cover it up."

I snap a couple photos and then cover it with some new stuff that we got. It's a waterproof clear bandage that she'll keep on for twenty-four hours, and then replace it with a new one after washing and keeping it there for three days.

"When you take this off, do it while you're in the shower; it'll be easier to get it off. If you need help putting it on tomorrow, just call us up and you can bring it in. One of us will be here to help you put it on."

She pays for her tattoo and gives me a hug before leaving. I clean up my station, singing along to a Pearl Jam song playing through the speakers.

"That tattoo turned out really, really well," Heidi says as she sits on my stool. "I wish I could do realism tattoos like you."

"I've been doing this a lot longer than you. You'll get there, and I can work with you if you want." We all have our strengths or the type of designs we'd rather do. I've always loved realism style. I've been working on a sketch of Iris that I want Sierra to do. It's a picture of Iris from her first birthday.

"Okay, sounds good." Heidi heads down the hall, and I finish cleaning.

I'm packing up my stuff for the day when my phone chirps. I pick it up and see a text from Joaquin.

Joaquin: I need to see you. Can you and Iris come over tonight for dinner?"

It warms me that he wants to see us.

Mona: We'll be there in a half hour.

I answer him and smile when he sends back a thumbs up.

In the office, Iris is sitting at the desk working on her homework. "Hey, sweetheart, are you about done?"

"Yep, give me two seconds."

I laugh because when Iris focuses on her work, she's got such a serious look on her face, and her tongue peeks out while she writes something on her paper. I wait patiently for her to finish. "Do you need me to look it over?"

Iris holds it out. I look it over, and it's simple addition; obviously, she *is* only seven. Of course, she got them all right because my girl is really good at math. I'm going to assume that she got that from Sam because math was always my worst subject.

"Looks great, baby. Get your stuff together; we're going to go have dinner at Joaquin and Max's."

It's comical how fast she gathers her papers and sticks them in her take-home folder. Hand in hand we step outside, and I get her settled in the backseat.

Twenty minutes later, we're pulling down the winding driveway. As soon as I throw the car into park, Iris is jumping out of the car and running full speed toward the front door. I'm climbing out just as Joaquin opens it.

My lady parts sing as I take in the fitted t-shirt, jeans, and bare feet. Iris runs right by him, yelling a quick "hello" before going after Max, I'm sure. Joaquin approaches and pulls me into his arms.

He leans down, kissing my lips slowly, and manages to make my toes curl. All too soon the kiss ends. "I'm glad you came," Joaquin says against my lips.

"Thanks for inviting us over."

He wraps his arm around my waist and leads me inside. I look around and then back at him. "Where's Victoria?"

"She's out with some sorority sisters of hers. I thought we could order take out, maybe Chinese?"

I hang my purse from the back of my chair at the kitchen island. Joaquin sits next to me with a menu in his hand. "I know what Max and I like; take a look and see what you and Iris would like."

He orders so much food I'm not sure we'll be able to eat it all. "It'll be here in about an hour." He grabs my hand. "Come with me." Joaquin leads me into the family room, and we sit on the sofa. I kick off my shoes, bring my legs up, and sit crisscross applesauce.

Joaquin hugs me to his side and kisses my temple. "How was your day?"

"It was good. I worked five hours on a really

special piece for a woman today. I'll show you a picture of it later. What about you?"

He grabs my arm and begins tracing Iris' name tattoo on my forearm. "My day was busy. I had back to back meetings, and then I met Nick for lunch. He's got it bad for your sister, and she keeps breaking things off."

I can only shake my head. "She had her heart broken in college, like bad, and ever since she's avoided relationships. Maybe he'll break the cycle. He seems like a good guy."

"He's my best friend, but I don't know if I'd call him relationship material. I'd just tell her to tread carefully. I love Nick and would do anything for him, but he's probably only still pursuing her because she keeps breaking things off with him. He loves a challenge." Joaquin hugs me to his side and keeps me there.

I rest my head on his shoulder and my hand on his hot freaking abs. "Umm ... my brother is going to keep Iris all weekend, and he offered to take Max too, so we could have some time to ourselves." I look up at him.

"Really?" Joaquin leans in, kissing my lips. "You and me alone for two days? We could have an amazing time—I can see it now, you, me, and no clothes."

I laugh. "You're bad, but that does sound really good. Miles is great with Iris. He'd take good care of Max."

"Baby, I believe you. Let's plan it then."

"Great, and if Victoria's going to be here, you could always come to my place. I know it's small compared to this place, but we'd have privacy." Ugh, I hate when I get self-conscious about stuff.

"I love your place, you know why?" I shake my head. "Because it's all you."

We're interrupted by the doorbell ringing. Joaquin goes to grab the food, and I pick up Fluffy who came running down the stairs as soon as the doorbell rang. He licks my hand when Joaquin comes walking in with two large bags of food, and it smells so good my mouth waters.

I kiss the top of the dog's head before setting him down. The kids come running into the room. "Guys, let's wash your hands." I lead them to the sink, and the three of us scrub them quick, and then I look to Joaquin. "Where do you want us?"

"Let's sit at the table. Do you want to grab some plates? Max, show Mona where the plates are." I follow the little cutie over to the cupboards, and he points to the one that contains the plates.

Once we've got the table set, Joaquin and I work side by side getting the kids set first. I place a couple veggie spring rolls and some veggie fried rice doused in soy sauce.

We're all silent at first while we eat, but it feels natural, right, all of us sitting together. The kids seem to be enjoying their food. I take a drink of my water. "Maximum, how's school?"

"It's okay. I'm pretty smart so it's easy, but it would be better if Iris was there with me." My daughter nods her agreement.

"I'm sorry, buddy, but she doesn't live here so she can't. She has to go to school by our house."

He seems to think about it for a moment. "She

can just move in here with us. You can come too."

"That's really sweet, honey, but we can't just move in with you so Iris can go to school with you."

I look at Joaquin and shake my head because both kids are pouting right now.

We finish the rest of dinner, and I help Joaquin clean up all of the trash off the table. The kids disappear upstairs. I stick all the leftovers into the refrigerator, close the door, and feel Joaquin come up behind me, and I lean into him as he wraps his arms around me.

He kisses behind my ear, causing goose bumps to pop up all over my body. This man can deduce me to a puddle of goo. I turn in his arms and pull his face to mine. Our kiss is hot and intense, but it ends all too soon.

The rest of the night is spent in front of the TV, watching The League reruns. I've never watched this before, but I'm going to have to start.

At eight o'clock, I call Iris down so we can leave. Both kids get a little attitude with us when we break the news. They hug each other, and then Max surprises me when he hugs me. I kiss the top of his head. "We'll see you in a couple of days, okay?"

"Yeah, okay."

Iris hugs Joaquin and then grabs my hand. We're to the door when I turn around. "Thank you for dinner."

He leans down and kisses me chastely on the lips in front of the kids. "Any time. Text me or call me to let me know you made it home.

The whole drive home I can't wipe the smile off of my face.

FOURTEEN

JOAQUIN

Mona shows me where to park in front of her brother's apartment building. I love my son, but I'm anxious for some alone time with my girl. Since we've become an us, the most we've done is kiss, and since I know what it feels like to be buried inside her, I miss it desperately.

I'm addicted to her; what can I say. I put the car in park and help Max hop out of the back, and I hand him his backpack with his clothes and toothbrush inside. Mona has Iris put her backpack on, and the kids walk hand in hand ahead of us.

Miles' doorman opens it for us, and Iris introduces Max to the older gentleman. My son has never met a stranger and takes the man's hand, shaking it. Iris and Max run to the elevator while Mona gives the man a hug.

Once inside the elevator Iris shows Max which button to press we ride it up to Miles's floor. The doors open and her brother appears in the doorway across from the elevator. "Hey, guys. Is this *the*

Maximum I've heard so much about?"

"That's me. You're tall! How come your hair isn't purple like Mona's?"

"*Mijo*, take a breath." I shake Miles' hand. "Thank you for offering to take him."

He claps me on the shoulder. "It's no trouble. I'm ahead on my word count and have lots of fun stuff planned. Our sister Heidi is coming over to hang with us too."

Miles gives me a tour of his apartment, and the place is fucking gorgeous. I'm sure he's paying a hefty price to live here, but when I see the view I'd pay whatever they asked. The skyline for downtown is gorgeous, and at night when it's all lit up it's phenomenal.

"This place is great." I grab my wallet out of my pocket. "Here's some money for whatever you guys do."

Miles immediately refuses, and before I can talk him into taking it, Mona and the kids find us. We only stay a few more minutes. The kids hug us goodbye just as Heidi comes walking in with pizza boxes. We're quickly pushed aside for pizza.

"We'll call the kids before bed," Mona tells her brother as we make our way toward the door.

"It's going to be fine. We're going to have some sick parties, maybe go clubbing, and hop a jet and maybe go to Vegas."

Mona slaps her brother and then hugs him and Heidi.

Once we're out in the hall, I swear my dick gets hard. We step onto the elevator, and she's immediately in my arms, my lips on hers. Our kiss is short but explosive. I just hope we can make it back to her place before we both explode.

Outside I help Mona into my Rover, and as soon as I climb inside her hand is immediately on my thigh, and I pull it right back off. "*Mi Cielo,* I can't have you touching me right now, or I may come like an inexperienced teenager."

"Oh, then I shouldn't tell you that I'm not wearing any panties." I push a little harder on the gas pedal as Mona chuckles beside me.

Against my better judgment, I reach over and put my hand on her thigh. I move it painfully slow up her smooth skin until I reach her cut-off jean shorts. I stroke the seam of her shorts that runs over her clit.

Mona gives a little moan and tries to shift away from me, but her seatbelt holds her captive. I increase the pressure, and her whimper has my cock ready to rip through my jeans. I glance at her from the corner of my eye and see that her eyes are closed and lips are parted.

The moment I turn down her street the sexual tension rises. I pull into her driveway, and in seconds we're jumping out of my Rover and hustling toward the house. I take the keys from her hand and quickly unlock the door.

She gasps as I pull her into the house, kick the door shut, and slam her against it. Our lips meet in an urgent kiss. I grab her ass, lifting her until her legs are wrapped around my waist.

I pull away from her reluctantly and quickly carry her down the hall while she nips at my earlobe, causing me to grunt. Once we're in her room, I set her down, grabbing her shirt, and ripping it up and off. I step back, taking a second to admire her beauty. "Fuck, you're so beautiful."

Mona moves closer to me, drops to her knees, and quickly undoes my jeans. The moment she frees my cock it starts leaking pre-cum. Her tongue comes out licking the head and moaning. The moment she engulfs me in her hot mouth I want to come, but I don't want to—I want to enjoy the feel of her mouth wrapped around me.

I grip her hair and fuck her mouth. The wet sounds of her mouth fill the room as she works my cock. That tingling at the base of my spine starts, but I'm not ready yet. I want to be balls deep inside her when I come.

I pull Mona off of my cock with a pop and toss her onto the bed. "Take off the rest of your clothes." My voice is deep, guttural.

She gets up on her knees and reaches behind her. Mona's bra straps fall down her shoulders. She gives me a coquettish smile as she lets her bra fall to the bed. I strip off my shirt, then pants and boxer briefs.

Mona stands up in the middle of her bed, and I'm mesmerized by her jiggling breasts while she works her shorts down her legs until she's finally naked. I lunge for her, taking her down onto her back.

She cries out in surprise, but that quickly changes to a moan when I lean down, sucking one nipple into my mouth. Mona's thighs hug my hips. She grips my hair in her fists as I suck the other nipple into my mouth, nipping the tip until she cries out.

I kiss my way down her body, nipping at her flesh until goose bumps pop up. The closer I get to her pussy, the more I can smell her arousal. My mouth waters with the desire to taste her.

Her pussy is covered by a tiny patch of blonde curls. I use my thumbs to open her up to me, lean forward, and lick her entrance up to her clit. Mona's grip on my hair tightens as I suck it into my mouth.

I thrust one finger inside her, then two, as I lick her clit. She moans loudly as I move my fingers in a come hither motion. The wet squelching sound bounces off the walls as she tightens around my fingers. I pull back, my eyes going to hers.

"Are you going to come for me, *mi cielo*?"

Mona nods, her hands going to her breasts, pinching and tugging at her nipples.

"Let me hear you." I rub her clit with the thumb of my other hand while rubbing the bundle of nerves on the inside. Her cries turn louder and more urgent.

The moment she comes, Mona soaks my hands and her back arches off the mattress. I slowly bring her down before pulling my fingers from her, licking her arousal off of my fingers.

I crawl up her body until my cock is at her entrance. After I convinced her to be an us again, I found out Mona was on birth control, and we were both clean so we decided that there would be nothing between us.

Now I'm eager to feel all of her. Holding up her leg by the thigh, I slowly push impossibly deep inside her. Both of us moan when I'm finally buried to the hilt. "Fuck, you're so hot, so tight."

We move together—her arm wraps around my neck, and our lips meet in a passionate dance. In no time I feel the beginning signs of Mona's orgasm. "Rub your clit, baby."

With her free hand, she reaches between us, stroking her clit until she comes again. She moans against my lips and then I increase my thrusts. "Oh fuck, I'm going to come." I bury myself to the hilt and shudder as I come violently inside her.

"Are you okay?" I whisper before kissing her lips. "I didn't hurt you, did I?"

Mona smiles up at me. "I'm great." She pushes my hair back.

I kiss her one more time before pulling out of her. "Good, I'll be right back. Don't. Get. Dressed."

"O ... K." She gives me a little salute that has me rolling her to her side, slapping her ass. "Owww ... jerkwad."

In the bathroom, I take care of business then wash my hands. I grab a washcloth, getting it wet before taking it back into the bedroom. I find Mona right where I left her. She grumbles when I insist on cleaning her up, but she gives in.

I toss the washcloth into the laundry basket in the corner and then lie down, pulling her into my arms. Our legs tangle together, and I kiss her forehead. Neither of us says a word as we snuggle, just enjoying the moment.

Mona's stomach growls and makes me laugh. "Does my girl need some food?"

"Feed me," she says in a singsong voice.

"It's probably best if we refuel because you're

going to need your strength." I pull her out of the bed and grab my boxer briefs, slipping them on. I grab my t-shirt and hand it to her. She slips it on and drowns in it, but there's just something so sexy about her being in my shirt.

She comes toward me. "Turn around."

I raise one brow, and she makes the hand gesture to turn around. I do what she says and feel her come up behind me. She places her hands on my shoulders, and I know what she's doing. "Hop on." I squat for her to hop on.

I carry her out to the kitchen and then set her down. "What are you feeding me?" I ask her.

"Iris and I had veggie quesadillas again. I could heat some up for us."

While the oven heats up, we make out like teenagers on the sofa with her cat watching us like a little stalker. Things become heated very quickly, and she rubs against my cock while straddling my lap until she comes with a surprised shout.

Mona slumps against my chest, and I wrap my arms around her, hugging her tight. When the oven beeps, she kisses me before climbing off and disappearing into the kitchen.

She comes back in carrying a couple beers. Mona crawls onto my lap and hands me mine. I wrap my arm around her, hugging her to my chest while taking a long pull of my beer.

"You haven't really talked about your parents. Are they still around?" I ask.

Mona takes a drink of her beer. "Oh yeah. My parents are great. They actually moved to Phoenix three years ago when my grandfather had a stroke.

Mom wanted to be close to the nursing home he lives in. My dad designs golf courses, and there are tons of those there." She smiles, "Mom's always been his right-hand gal. They usually come for a couple weeks around Christmas, and they spoil Iris rotten. I know you said that your parents are divorced, but are you close?"

I shrug because I never know how to answer this. "Yes, no, or maybe. Things between my dad and I are better now that I'm older, and he's okay with Max, but we're not like other families. I'm definitely closer to my mom, but she's enjoying the jet-setting lifestyle with her husband when they're not fighting, and I rarely see her. She's as much of a grandma as Melina is a mother."

"I'm sorry." She wraps her arms around my head, hugging me to her breasts.

"Baby, don't be sorry. It is what it is, but those are the reasons I've tried very hard to do things differently with Max."

She kisses my cheek. "I know I've said it before, but you're a really good dad."

"Well, I think you're a phenomenal mom."

"We definitely rock." Mona holds her beer bottle up to mine, and we clink them together.

The timer dings, and she climbs off of my lap and disappears into the kitchen. "Do you need my help in there?"

"Nope, I've got it covered."

Mona returns a few minutes later with plates full of food. She hands my plate to me and sits next to me. We're quiet while we eat, and I realize that I'm more relaxed than I think I've ever been.

I open my eyes and find Mona's side of the bed empty. When I reach out and touch it, it feels cool. I grab her pillow and bring it to my face, taking in her sweet scent.

If it's possible, I think my dick is broken. Last night after dinner and a quick call to check on the kids, I was loading plates into the dishwasher when Mona came up behind me, wrapping her arms around me. I thought she was just hugging me, but then she shoved her hand in my jeans and then my underwear, wrapping her hand around my dick.

She jerked my cock until I came with a shout. I grabbed her and threw her over my shoulder and carried her to her bedroom, eating her pussy until she came twice on my tongue.

We took a little nap before I woke Mona up with my tongue between her legs again, and then I fucked her slowly and thoroughly until we were both on the verge of coming. I then flipped us so she was riding me—fucking herself on my dick until we came together.

We finally fell asleep after one in the morning. After I got up to use the bathroom at six, I fucked Mona, both of us on our sides—my chest snug against her back as I held her leg up to fuck her slowly.

I sit up and look down. "No," I tell my dick that's hard from just thinking about her. I grab my bag and pull out a pair of basketball shorts and throw them on. In the bathroom, I take care of business and then brush my teeth before heading out into the living room.

Soft music drifts down the hall the closer I get to the living room, a unique scent floats through the air, and my girl is sitting on a little pillow with her legs crossed and her palms resting on her thighs.

I smile when I find Peanut sitting in front of Mona just staring at her. Since she's meditating, I walk quietly into the kitchen and see an almost full pot of coffee. I pour myself a cup and take a sip, letting the hot brew help clear the cobwebs from my brain.

Mona comes into the kitchen and comes right to me. "Good morning." She kisses my lips before she grabs a cup, filling it with coffee.

"Morning, *mi cielo*. How was your meditation?"

"It was great. Since I've started meditating I love starting my day that way. Hell, I love ending my day that way too. It's just a good way to clear my head and push away any negative thoughts polluting my mind." She shakes her head and laughs softly. "I know that probably sounds hokey, but it's just a little me time."

"It doesn't sound hokey. It's good that you take care of yourself." I set my coffee down, then take hers and do the same. I pull her into my arms. "What do you say we go grab some breakfast. Then we'll go to the store and get some provisions, then come back here and spend the rest of the weekend naked." I kiss behind her ear.

"That sounds amazing, especially the naked part." Mona gives me a saucy wink.

I scoop her up in my arms. "We better go shower then, so we can get clean."

Needless to say, our shower got us dirty before we could get clean.

#

MONA

Joaquin grabs my hand and brings it to his lips, kissing the back of it. We're on our way to pick up the kids from my brother's. I'm sad that our weekend is almost over, but I think this is just what we needed. Now I feel like I know him a lot more.

"I had such an amazing weekend." I smile at him from the passenger seat.

He kisses my hand again. "I did too. Maybe next time we can take the kids somewhere for an overnight trip, or do you think it's too soon." Joaquin glances at me and then back at the road.

"I don't think it's too soon. The kids know we're together. They'd probably love a weekend getaway."

Joaquin pulls up in front of Miles' building. He comes around and opens the door for me. Once he shuts and locks it, he wraps his arm around my waist as we make our way inside.

As soon as we step off the elevator, the door to

my brother's apartment opens, and my daughter comes running toward me. I squat and open my arms. She hits my body and sends me to my back. "Hi, my sweet girl; did you miss me?"

"No, we had too much fun." Iris giggles. "Just kidding."

I get up and hug Max as he comes running to me. "Hey, buddy. How was your weekend? Did you make sure Miles behaved?"

"Yep, Iris and I made sure he was good." The sweet boy goes to his dad who picks him up in his arms and hugs him tight.

We step inside Miles' apartment, and Nerf darts litter the floor. I'm sure there were plenty of battles this weekend.

"Kids, why don't you pick up the darts for Miles," Joaquin says. Both kids hop to it. "I hope he was okay for you," he says to my brother.

"He was great. They did get into quite a heated argument last night about what movie to watch, so I made the decision for them. We swam yesterday, and Greta came over to join us. Sierra and Heidi were both busy at the studio."

Joaquin nods. "I'm glad he was good and had a good time. I can't thank you enough for keeping them."

I get the kids' stuff together while Miles and Joaquin talk books. My brother shows him the bookshelves that are filled with his crime series. They talk animatedly as Joaquin pulls out different books from the shelves, and they both look at the back covers.

By the time I have the kids' bags by the door,

they've cleaned up the Nerf stuff and put the pillows back on the sofa. "Guys, go get your shoes on."

It takes a good ten minutes before we're finally ready to go. The kids grumble on our way out to the SUV. Once we get back to my house, I help Iris down while Joaquin grabs her backpack.

He stops on the sidewalk and pulls me into his arms. "I wish the weekend wasn't over. What am I going to do without you?"

My belly warms at his words, and I want to climb his body so bad right now.

Joaquin shakes his head. "Don't look at me like that," he says quietly. "Now kiss me, and get your girl inside."

I reach up on my tiptoes and press my lips to his. It's a quick kiss, but it'll do for now. I step away from him and pull open Max's door. "I'll see you later, Maximum." My favorite little boy gives me a quick hug and then shouts his goodbye to Iris.

Butterflies begin to take flight in my belly when Iris jumps at Joaquin. He scoops her up in his arms and hugs her tight. "I'll see you later, *preciosita.*" Iris surprises us both when she leans in and kisses his cheek.

She gives him a huge smile. "Bye, Joaq." Joaquin sets her down, and she screams bye to Max through the window.

I step in close to Joaquin till our chests almost touch. "Thank you for an incredible weekend."

He leans in and kisses my forehead. "I should be thanking you. I'll talk to you later."

Iris and I walk hand in hand up to the door.

Joaquin honks his horn and gives us a wave before he pulls away and disappears down the street. I let us in and tell Iris to go put her dirty clothes into the basket and to put her toothbrush back in the cup holder.

Peanut comes out to greet me and meows as he weaves between my legs. I pick him up and give him some love before placing him on the ground and grabbing him a couple of the kitty treats that he loves.

While he eats those, Iris comes running into the kitchen. "What's for dinner?"

"Well, I thought we could do grilled cheese sandwiches and steamed broccoli." Which is her favorite. "We can watch some Fuller House too."

She does a little happy dance and then runs into the living room with Peanut following behind her.

I have a feeling tonight is going to be an early bedtime for both of us.

I pull into the driveway of the huge pretentious McMansion that I'm not surprised Sam lives in. We're here today for Iris to meet her sister who is a week old. I honestly was surprised that Sam called to tell his daughter the news, but he did.

He and I haven't spoken about the party incident, or him showing up at my place and Joaquin having to step in—standing up for Iris and me. When he calls, he asks to speak to Iris, but that's fine with me.

I shut the car off and climb out, walking around

174

to help Iris out. My sweet daughter picked out a baby gift and holds it proudly on her lap. We walk up to the door as it opens. Sam greets us, looking tired and stressed. "Hiya, Sam," Iris says and holds up her bag. "I brought my sister a present."

"That's nice. Come on in." A baby screams from somewhere in this huge ass house. Iris vibrates with excitement to see her.

We follow Sam through a formal type living room, the kitchen, and into what appears to be a family room. His wife sits on the sofa, and their son sits on the floor playing with a truck.

"Hi, Tawney. Where's my sister? Hey Nixon." The little boy ignores Iris and neither of his parents correct his rude behavior, but whatever; he's not my child.

"She's with the nanny having her diaper changed."

I'm biting my tongue so hard right now to keep from saying something snarky. Iris carries the bag to Tawney and hands it to her. "Here's a present. I made it myself."

The woman—who looks too put together for just having a baby, but I guess she's probably well rested having someone help her and all—gives my daughter a fake smile. Ugh, that's mean; I should stop. An older woman walks in with a tiny pink bundle in her arms. She hands the baby to Tawney and then disappears.

Iris tentatively walks forward. She's been around some babies, but not a lot, and I don't even think she's held one. "She's so pretty." She smiles over her shoulder at me. "Was I this tiny?"

I nod, ignoring how uncomfortable Sam looks. It's not my fault he bailed before Iris was born. "You were. She's really beautiful," I say, looking at Tawney.

She smiles, but again it's totally fake. "Thank you."

"Can I hold her?" Iris vibrates with excitement. She moves closer to Tawney with the biggest smile on her face.

My spine immediately stiffens when Tawney's face scrunches up. "Umm … you need to wash your hands first."

"I washed them before we came. Didn't I, Mommy?" she says as she turns to me. Iris holds up them up. "They're clean; I promise."

"Iris, let's go wash your hands. We don't want the baby to get sick." I look at Sam. "Where's the bathroom?"

He leads us around the corner to a little half bath. I take Iris inside and shut the door and squat in front of her. "Sometimes we can carry little germies that we miss when washing our hands. We want to make sure we protect the little ones."

That makes her feel a little better, and she quickly scrubs her hands clean. We head into the family room, and Iris sits next to Tawney, and I sit on her other side. As soon as the baby is placed in my daughter's arms, she smiles so brightly that I'm practically blinded by it.

"What's her name?" I ask.

"Her name is Nicole, after Sam's grandmother." Tawney picks up the gift bag and pulls the paper out and then the picture frame that Iris made for the baby. Her school picture is in the frame. "Ohhh … this is … nice. I know just where to put this." She sticks it back in the bag and sets it aside like it's nothing.

We don't stay long after that. I don't know if I'm being overly sensitive, but Tawney was cold toward my daughter, and I didn't like that at all. Sam walked us out and didn't even try to make plans to see Iris again. All he said was he'd call her.

Now we're on our way to pick up Max, then going to a movie and out for dinner. Joaquin is going with Nick to tour the indoor football arena for the team he's going to co-own. Victoria has plans, so we're going to get our buddy and then spend the evening with him until Joaquin gets done with Nick.

We arrive at Joaq's, and Iris walks toward the door with a lot less enthusiasm than she usually has when we come to see Max. I know what dulled my baby's light, and my stomach knots just thinking about it.

Maybe it's time to cut off visits for a while, but if I do that Sam could possibly get a lawyer and fight for joint or shared custody. It can't be healthy for Iris if she's getting so quiet, almost depressed after visits with *those* people.

Victoria opens the door. "Hi, Iris." My daughter gives her a quiet 'hey' and walks into the house. She leans in and asks, "Is Iris okay? Joaquin said you guys went to see her new baby sister today. Did it not go well?"

I step inside, and she leads me into the kitchen. "It was weird, and then it was awkward." I tell her about everything, and by the time I'm done, my eyes are filling with unshed tears. "I'm sorry; I don't know why I'm crying." Victoria hands me a tissue.

"You're crying because you love your daughter very much and don't ever want anything to hurt her." She pulls me into a hug. "I'll tell you the same thing I told my cousin. That little girl is going to be just fine, and that's because she's got a mom who will protect her with everything she's got."

"Thank you so much for talking me down from the emotional ledge. I just wish we'd never seen him that day, but you're right. I will protect her until my last dying breath."

Victoria glances at her phone. "I've got to go. I'm meeting some friends, but here are the keys to the house. Joaquin wanted you to have these so you could come back here if you want." She hands me the set of keys, and when I see the keyring, I smile. It's a silver tattoo machine and looks just like the one I first used when I did tattoos.

She leans in. "He had that specially made for you."

Warmth fills my belly, and my heart beats rapidly in my chest. "Thank you." That's all I can say because I'm ready to cry, again.

Victoria kisses my cheek, hollers a goodbye to the kids, and leaves.

It feels weird being in Joaquin's home without him here. I make my way upstairs and find the kids lying across Max's bed, and he's reading a book out loud to her. Fluffy is snuggled up in between the kids and barely lifts his head acknowledging me standing here.

I walk further into the room, and my daughter looks up at me and smiles. It's not filled with the same brightness that it usually is, but I'll get her there. I'm sure the little boy next to her will ensure that as well.

"Are you guys ready to go have some fun?" I jump up and down and clap.

Of course, both kids look at me like I'm cuckoo. I dance around like a clown, and the kids laugh.

My girl's sweet giggle makes me so fucking happy.

MONA

Mona

I wasn't ready to head back to Joaquin's, so I decided to bring the kids to Jumping Joe's. I sent Joaquin a text letting him know just in case he got home before us. I watch the kids jump around at the trampoline park and tire themselves out. Every time they call for me, I paste on my best fake smile and watch them jump and flip around. My stomach twists as I look down at my phone.

I was scanning Instagram a few minutes ago and saw a picture that Nick had posted. It was him, Joaquin, and another guy all cheesing it up for the camera and surrounded by the cheerleaders for the Atlanta Fire.

They were all in tiny sports bras, showcasing large, perky breasts, and bootie shorts showing off flat abs and long legs. Joaquin hasn't given me any reason not to trust him, but that doesn't mean I'm not jealous. I could never compete with those girls—I've had a child and even though I'm thin, she still changed my body.

Some of the comments make my stomach hurt. There's a lot of, *I hope you're banging at least one of them*. A lot of, *you're the luckiest men alive*. Others say stuff that I don't care to repeat.

I stick the phone in my purse and focus on the kids.

"Mona, come jump with us," Max hollers from the other side of the trampoline he and Iris are jumping on.

I slip off my shoes and tuck them under our bench. "Scoot back, kids, and I'll show you how it's done." They cheer me on as I bounce up and down. Once I catch some good air, I do a backflip, happy that I land on my feet.

"That was awesome, Mom." My daughter's excitement makes me smile. "Do it again."

"Yeah do it, Mona," Max shouts.

I bounce again and do a flip. I step off to the side to catch my breath and give the kids a chance to jump. They hold hands as they fly up and down, squealing in delight.

They stop, and Iris screeches. "Joaq." I freeze and turn to find my daughter launching herself at Joaquin. He catches her with no problem and hugs her tight. He whispers something in her ear, and she nods before kissing his cheek.

Max runs to his dad, and I find Nick walking toward us. I don't miss that all of the women, young and old, are checking both men out. They look like they should be modeling really expensive menswear.

They're dressed alike, in dress pants that fit like they were tailored especially for them. My eyes immediately go to the bulge in Joaquin's pants, and my heart starts to race. They're wearing dress shirts tucked into their pants and no tie. Nick's shirt is a crisp white, and Joaquin's is a slate gray.

I realize what I'm wearing and suddenly feel very self-conscious. I'm in worn, holey cut-off jean shorts, my old Duran Duran t-shirt. My hair is in a haphazard ponytail. The women from the picture I saw earlier flashes through my mind, and nausea curdles in my belly.

What is wrong with me? Joaquin looks up and catches my eye. He smiles, but then it falls.

Joaquin holds his hand out to me, and I take it. He pulls me toward him. The height of the trampoline is low enough that we're eye to eye. "Are you okay?"

I shrug. My eyes burn, and I quickly blink to stop it.

"Baby, go grab your shoes." He turns to Nick. "Keep an eye on the kids for a minute."

After slipping my shoes on, Joaquin leads me outside and to a bench to sit. He wraps his arm around my shoulders, hugging me into his side. "What happened at Sam's today?"

I rest my head on his shoulder and tell him all about it and my worries. "I just felt no love in that house. Maybe it was just because Iris was there, but it felt so cold." I look up at him. "Her own brother didn't want anything to do with her, and little ones love her. You should've seen her with her sister. It was so sweet, and every time she would talk to her, her eyes would open, and she'd just stare up at her."

Joaquin places his lips against my forehead. "I'm sorry it wasn't the experience you were hoping for. How was Iris after you left?"

"She was quiet, withdrawn. That amazing little boy of yours knows exactly how to make my girl smile."

We're quiet as we stare out across the parking lot. "Did you have a good time with Nick? The pictures on Instagram were good." I practically choke on those words because I feel like a jealous cow.

"I did. It was pretty cool to see behind the scenes. The cheerleaders were there practicing, and Nick just *had* to get a picture with them."

"They were all so beautiful."

He squeezes me. "They were, but they don't hold a candle to this lavender-haired, tattoo-covered hottie who makes me hard every time I look at her." Joaquin kisses behind my ear. "You have nothing to worry about. I *want* you."

"Sorry, I didn't mean to be all Debbie Downer. It's just been a really weird day." I cup his cheek and kiss him slowly, chastely. We end our kiss sooner than I'd like, and he grabs my hand, and we head back inside.

We find Nick jumping on the trampoline with the kids, and it's quite the sight. The man is huge but bouncing up and down like he's a giant child. They notice us walking up, and the blond hops down and picks me up, hugging me tightly. "Hey, beautiful."

"Hey yourself." I smile down at him.

"Nick, please put my girlfriend down before I beat you up in front of all these people."

My cheeks warm because this is the first time he's called me his girlfriend. Nick sets me down and grabs my forearms, holding them out. "You Collins women are gorgeous, especially this one." He picks up Iris. "Iris, you look just like your momma."

"I know, and when I get bigger I can have lavender hair too."

We don't stay much longer before the five of us head outside. The kids look tired, but they did jump a lot tonight. I'm not sure if I'm supposed to take Max with me or not, so we head toward my car.

"I'll talk to you later." I hear Joaquin say from behind me. Then I feel his hand on my lower back. "Hand me your keys, *mi cielo.*"

Joaquin has called me that several times. I haven't looked up the meaning yet, maybe because I'm scared of what it means. Is it something that is going to make me fall in love with him? Who am I kidding; I'm already falling.

I hand him the keys, and he keeps hold of my hand, pulling me toward him. He takes my lips in a searing kiss as Iris "Awwwws," and Max says, "Gross."

Joaquin laughs against my lips. "Let's get out of here."

We get the kids settled in the backseat and climb in, heading back to his house. Once there, we head inside and Joaquin turns on a movie for the kids who lay down on the floor in front of the TV. He grabs a bottle of wine, two wine glasses, and whistles for the dog to follow us outside.

While Fluffy runs around and does his business, Joaquin pours us both a glass of wine and hands me one. I take a sip, and the dry fruity flavor hits my tongue, and I moan. After today I totally need this.

Once the dog is ready to go inside, Joaquin gets up and lets him in, checking on the kids before coming back out. He pulls me to him, and I snuggle in close. "Thank you for keeping Max today."

"Of course, anytime. What are the kids doing?"

Joaquin places his lips against my temple and inhales. "They're both asleep. I threw a blanket over them. They wore themselves out." He pulls his phone out and presses a couple of buttons, and soft music floats across the backyard.

"The nights are becoming cooler." I snuggle deeper into his side. I drain the last of my wine and lean forward, setting the glass on the little table.

"They are." He turns so he's facing me more. "I wanted to run something by you. What do you think about you and Iris spending the night here sometimes? There's a bedroom next to Max's that's empty right now. I know during the week it would be too hard because of Iris' school, but on the weekends I want my girls here."

Butterflies take flight in my belly. I can't believe he wants us here in his space, that he's got a room for my daughter to stay in—that he wants her to stay in. "Really? That's really sweet. Don't you think it's too soon?"

Joaquin sifts his hand through my hair and grabs me, lifting me until I'm straddling his lap. "No, I don't. I've never been surer of anything."

"What about Victoria? I don't want to feel like

I'm encroaching on her space." I know the house is Joaquin's, but she's stayed with him to help with his son. While she lives here, it's her space too.

"She's never here during the weekends. Usually, she's with friends or a boyfriend, if she has one. Plus, my cousin loves you and Iris."

I lean down and kiss his lips then pull back. "Okay, but I need to talk to Iris about it. I just want to make sure she's okay with this."

Joaquin pulls me down, kissing my lips. "Of course. Max and I have already talked about the possibility of it, and he is down for it."

All of me by John Legend starts playing, and he stands me up. For a second I think we're heading inside; instead, Joaquin grabs me and we slow dance under the stars. I'm not even surprised he's a good dancer as he gracefully moves me around the patio.

The moment the song ends, his lips are on mine. We meet in a fiery glide that makes my toes curl. Our tongues duel, and I moan into his mouth. He picks me up with ease, and I wrap my legs around his waist.

"Let's go inside," he whispers against my mouth. Joaquin sets me down, grabs my hand, and pulls me inside. He quickly locks the back door and then the front before setting the alarm.

We pass by the kids who are sleeping soundly. Fluffy is curled up against Iris' stomach. That's our cat's favorite spot to snuggle with her as well. We reach his room and step inside. Joaquin locks the door, and my breasts begin to tingle.

"Can you be quiet?"

I narrow my eyes at him. "I'm not loud."

Joaquin comes toward me until we're standing chest to chest. "Oh, baby, you moan so loud the moment I slide inside you, and I really fucking love it."

I can't even deny it because it's so true. I've never been as vocal as I am with him. He makes me feel wild and uninhibited. "I promise I'll be quiet."

He tosses me on the bed then pulls his shirt off and throws it on the chair in the corner, followed by his pants, boxer briefs, and socks. Like a panther, he stalks toward me, and my legs fall open, welcoming him between them.

Joaquin unbuttons my shorts and pulls them and my panties off. I quickly pull my shirt off and unhook my bra. "We have to be quick just in case the kids wake up," he whispers before sucking one nipple into his mouth.

I cover my mouth with one hand as I moan against it. He chuckles softly as he moves from one nipple to the other. His hair is soft beneath my fingers. Joaquin moans as he reaches in between us, fingering my pussy.

"I love how wet you get for me." He removes his finger and then sucks it into his mouth. "You taste so sweet."

I reach between us and wrap my hand around his stiff length. My thumb is coated in pre-cum as I drag it across the tip. I lean up, pressing my lips to his ear. "Fuck me, baby."

He grabs his cock and rubs it through my wetness. Joaquin lines up and starts to work himself inside of me. The moment he buries himself to the

188

hilt, he covers my mouth with his. My pussy spasms around his stiff length as he pulls almost all the way out and then thrusts inside me.

The desire to come hits me hard. Joaquin grabs my thigh, lifting it higher, and grinds against my clit until I come. He kisses me as he fucks me harder and harder.

I feel it the moment he comes inside me. Every hot pulse sends shockwaves through my body. When he finally collapses on top of me, I wrap my arms and legs around him.

"Am I squishing you?"

I kiss his neck. "No, I like it."

Joaquin pulls out and kisses me before climbing out of the bed. He disappears inside his bathroom, and I bury my nose in his pillow, inhaling his masculine scent. He steps into the bedroom and climbs on the bed. I let him clean me off. After tossing the washcloth in the basket, he climbs back into bed.

We snuggle chest to chest and our legs tangled together. "Do you guys want to stay tonight? I'd feel better if you didn't drive home this late at night. Plus, Iris is knocked out. If you think it'd be better, we can go sleep on the sectional. We'd both fit."

I love that he's so concerned about my safety. "We'll stay. I think it will be okay if we sleep in here as long as we have clothes on. Maybe I'll go wake her to go to the bathroom then let her go back to sleep."

"Let's go wake them up, then we'll get them settled on the sectional." I slip on my t-shirt sans bra and a pair of his basketball shorts. I, of course, have to fold them over multiple times to get them to fit … sort of.

It takes us about ten minutes to get the kids wrangled into the bathroom. Joaquin grabs me a spare toothbrush for Iris. The kids are happy about having the sleepover, and in no time we're tucking them in on the sectional with Fluffy sleeping in between them.

I bend down and kiss my daughter's forehead. "Night, baby. I love you."

Her slender arms wrap around my neck, and Iris hugs me tightly to her. "I love you, Mommy." Iris holds out her arms to Joaquin. My heart swells as my daughter hugs him, and he tenderly kisses her forehead. "Night, Joaq."

"Goodnight, *preciosita.*"

"My turn, Mona." Max holds his arms out to me. I bend down, hugging him and kissing the top of his head. "I had fun today."

"I had fun today too, sweetheart. I'll see you in the morning, okay?" He nods, and I stand.

"Night, *mijo.*" Joaquin dims the light in the family room so it's a faint glow, grabs my hand, and pulls me down the hall to his room.

The moment he shuts the door, Joaquin grabs me and slams me into the wall, his lips landing on mine. The kiss is deep and brutal. He lifts me again and presses me into the wall and grinds his dick against me. We move again until my back hits his mattress, and he's between my legs.

"What was that?" I whisper.

He brushes my hair out of my face and shakes his head. "Just seeing you with my son. It's so clear that you care about him. It just … it just makes me happy that he has that. That we found you and Iris."

That is the sweetest thing that someone has ever said to me. The butterflies in my stomach take flight. "Of course, I care about him. I'm falling in love with his dad." I freeze because I swore I was just thinking that and didn't actually say it out loud.

He freezes above me, and I want to crawl under his bed and hide. "I didn't mean it. It was just sweet what you said…"

Joaquin covers my mouth with his hand. "Shhh … I'm falling in love with you too."

My eyes burn, and I quickly blink before tears start to fall. He pulls his hand away and kisses me. It doesn't take long before things become heated. It's a long time before we finally fall asleep, dressed of course, but completely entangled with each other.

SEVENTEEN

JOAQUIN

A month has gone by since I asked Mona and Iris to stay with us on the weekends. After our first sleepover, Mona had asked her daughter how she felt about coming to stay with us on the weekends and the four of us being together. That little angel was thrilled.

Even if Mona has to go into the studio on a Saturday, Iris still stays with us unless she's spending time with one of her aunts or her uncle. Tonight, when they come over, I've got a surprise for Iris—Mona too, since I didn't tell her what I was doing.

See, I wanted to do something special for that sweet little girl because that asshole father of hers hasn't tried to see her since the baby was born. At first, he called her a couple times a week to talk about school, the other kids, and whatever Iris wanted.

Now she hasn't heard from him in a week and a

half. Mona even called him and left a voicemail asking for him to call and still nothing. It's starting to wear on Mona and affecting Iris.

I shake out my hands that I realize are clenched in tight fists.

"Dad?" Max calls from the hall.

I take a deep breath. "In here, *mijo*."

Max comes in and stands next to me. I know what he's seeing: pink and lavender striped walls. I didn't think they'd look good, but Victoria was right; it was the perfect choice. A full-size bed is in the corner of the room with a white headboard. The bedding is lavender with butterflies all over them.

We found a giant unicorn decal that we put on the wall. Victoria went a little crazy with draping twinkle lights across the ceiling. It's a total girly girl room and looks like it belongs to Iris.

"What do you think, bud? Will Iris like this room?"

He nods. "Definitely. Did you see the R2D2 lights that Victoria got for me? They're so cool."

My *prima* loves to spoil my child and does it often. "I didn't. Show me." I follow him down the hall and into his room and, sure enough, the lights are strung across his room, casting a whitish-blue glow. His room is all Star Wars, all the time. "This looks great, buddy. After dinner, I'll help you with your homework."

We head downstairs, and I make us a couple of grilled cheese sandwiches and bowls of fruit. Since it's just the two of us, we sit at the island. "Halloween's coming up. Have you thought about what you want to be?"

He nods while shoving a huge chunk of cantaloupe into his mouth. Once he chews and swallows it down, he looks at me. "I want to be a stormtrooper."

"Okay, we'll have to go shopping for your costume."

"I tried to get Iris to be Ren, but she said she's gonna be a stupid unicorn butterfly." He sticks his tongue out and makes a gagging sound.

"Hey, it's not stupid. She can be whatever she wants; what if she asked you to be a unicorn bumblebee? Would you do it if you didn't want to?"

Max shakes his head. "No, I guess not."

We finish eating, and I quickly clean up our mess. At the table, I watch him do his homework. I pay a lot for him to go to the private school he attends, and it's been money well spent. He's in a smaller class and gets more one on one attention. If I knew Mona would accept it, I'd pay for Iris to attend too.

My phone rings, and I see my father's face pop up. I squeeze my eyes shut because I'm not in the mood for this, but I know if I don't answer, then he'll continue to call until I do.

"Hello, Dad. How are you?" Max looks up at me and then back at his spelling words.

"Good. I wanted to let you know that I'll be coming to town at the beginning of next month. I want you to plan a family dinner while I'm there. Have it catered or hire someone to come cook it. When you get it figured out, just send me the bill and I'll pay for it." Dad says something to someone in the background.

I shake my head because even at thirty he still loves telling me what to do. "I'll arrange it. You'll get the chance to meet my girlfriend."

"Your girlfriend? Since when do you have girlfriends? Every time I've tried to set you up with someone you refuse me."

Fuck me, he always tries to set me up as part of some deal he's trying to make, a colleague's single daughter or some other relation. Yes, my father retired, but he's got his hands in so many businesses he works just as much, if not more, than he did before.

"Her daughter is Max's best friend; that's how we met. She's incredible." I don't tell him about the tattoos or lavender hair—it'll piss me off if he talks shit about her. I want him to meet her and see how amazing she is before he knows what she does for a living.

"Hmmm ... well, I look forward to meeting her. I'll have a car pick me up, and I'm staying at the Four Seasons. Hillary will send you the information. I'll talk to you next week." Just like that, he hangs up. Always in a rush to get off the phone.

I want to roll my eyes at the mention of Hillary. Shortly after my divorce, my father came to town with his "assistant". She'd come on to me and it had been a while, so I fucked her.

First, it was the worst sex I've ever had—she basically laid there and expected me to do all of the work. Second, I found out that she's my father's occasional side piece, and I didn't appreciate sticking my dick somewhere that my dad had been.

"Is Grandpa coming to visit?" My father loves

his grandson, but he's not real grandfatherly.

"Yeah, *mijo*, he'll be here after Halloween."

The moment I hear the front door open, Max and I head to the foyer. We find Mona and Iris stepping inside. "Hey, guys." Mona comes to me and kisses me soundly on the lips.

"Hey, baby. I've missed you." Her smile lights up her whole face.

Iris comes over and wraps his arms around my waist. "Hey, Joaq."

"Hi, *preciosita.* We have a surprise for you, but you and your mom need to wear these." I hold up two blindfolds.

Mona raises a brow and asks, "What is it?"

I shake my head. "Nope, you're going to have to wait and see it together." I tie the blindfolds over their eyes, and then we lead them upstairs. Iris' nervous giggles make me smile.

Max is smiling so wide when we lead them into Iris' new room. "Okay, before I take the blindfolds off, I want to say we did this so Iris would feel more at home when you guys spend the weekend with us. Iris, are you ready?"

She hops up and down. "I'm ready, I'm ready."

I nervously step behind Mona and untie her blindfold, and as soon as she sees the room, she covers her mouth with her hand. Next, I step behind Iris and take hers off. The moment she looks around and sees what we've done, she freezes.

Fuck, I don't think she likes it. I stand in front of

her and squat. "Sweetheart, if you don't like it, I can redo it and make it something you like."

Iris shakes her head. "It's the prettiest room I've ever seen." She throws herself at me and begins to cry. "Thank you." Her tears wet my neck, and I look up at Mona who has her arm around Max. She's smiling, but I don't miss the tears that leak from her eyes.

I stand up easily with Iris still wrapped around me, hugging me tightly. Mona and Max join us, and this moment right here, right now, is the moment that I know I'm in love with both of my girls.

Once Iris stops crying, I set her down, and Mona wraps her arms around my waist. She rests her head on my shoulder while we watch Max go over every little detail about Iris' room with her. "You're an amazing man, Joaquin Pena."

"Let's leave them to it, and you can help me start dinner." I lead her to the door. "Kids, we'll be downstairs."

In the kitchen, Mona cuts up vegetables while I cook chicken for Max and me. That's been a challenge, they're vegetarians, and Max and I are not. Most of the time we make two versions of the same dinner.

Mona wraps her arms around my waist and kisses the middle of my back. "I still can't believe what you did for Iris." Her voice cracks.

I turn and pull her around to my front. "No tears, *mi cielo*. We just wanted her to feel comfortable when she spends the night." She meets me halfway when I lean down to kiss her. I moan as our tongues do a little dance. My fingers sift through her lavender locks. I grip a chunk of hair at the base of her skull and deepen the kiss.

A timer goes off, and I reluctantly pull away from her. "Let's continue *that* conversation later." I lean down and kiss behind her ear.

"It's a date."

Mona goes up to get the kids, and I make the kids' plates, carrying them to the table. The three of them come into the kitchen, and the kids sit at the table.

Once we're all settled at the table, the kids dig in. I take a bite of my chicken and look at Mona. "My dad's coming into town right after Halloween. He's looking forward to meeting you."

Her eyes widen in surprise. "You want me to meet your dad?"

I know she said she didn't have a great experience with Sam's father. She never did tell me what the man said to her the day Iris went to that party, and Mona had to pick her up. "Of course, I do. I want him to meet both of you. He wants to have a dinner party here. I'm supposed to either hire a caterer or have someone come to the house to cook."

"Well, that's silly I could cook the meal. It'd be a lot cheaper, and I love to cook. Maybe Victoria could help me."

"Baby, that's really sweet to offer, but my father is a total meat and potatoes kind of guy." I'm afraid he'd laugh if she tried to feed him one of her vegetarian dishes.

"You do know I used to eat meat, right? I can cook just about anything as long as I have a recipe.

Let me do this, please."

I grab her hand and bring it to my lips. "Okay, baby. You can cook." I kiss it before letting go and go back to eating.

After dishes and getting the kids in their jammies, Mona and I snuggle on the sectional while the kids lie on the floor with Fluffy, and we watch the first Transformers movie. The kids fall asleep about an hour into it.

We talk quietly in between kisses. Mona's sitting across my lap, and we have a blanket over us. "Is your studio open on Halloween?" I ask quietly.

"No, we usually close early so my sisters can go trick-or-treating with Iris and me. Why?" She plays with my hair in the back.

"I was thinking your brother and sisters could come over for a mini-party and then we could take the kids trick-or-treating. Victoria will be here, and maybe Nick will come too. We could do snacks, and when it's time for trick-or-treating to start, maybe a couple of them would be willing to pass out candy while we're out." I rub my hand up and down her silky, smooth thigh.

"Are you going to dress up?" Mona asks before kissing my lips. "Sexy pirate? Naughty cop? Prison inmate?"

I shake my head. "I'm going to be just plain, sexy old me." I give her my best panty-dropping smile.

Her cheeks turn pink—I just made her blush. I reach out and rub my thumb across her flushed skin. I place my lips against Mona's ear. "I need you naked. Meet me in bed in five minutes. I'm going to make sure the house is locked up and the alarm is set." I help her off the couch and kiss her. "If you're not naked, I will turn that luscious ass red."

I don't miss her licking her lips and eyeing me up and down. I lunge for her, but she takes off running, her laughter drifting through the house. After covering the kids with blankets, I lock up the house and set the alarm.

On the way to my room, my dick gets hard. Is she going to be naked, or is she going to be naughty and make me spank her? I take a deep breath and open the door. I find my girl in the middle of the bed, and I quickly shut and lock the door. "Oh, baby, get that ass in the air."

Mona immediately bends over, shaking her ass at me. Fuck, she is so sexy. I pull off my shirt and take off my jeans, leaving me in just my boxer briefs. She looks behind her and smiles.

I'm a lucky fucking man.

The sun shines brightly in my room. I roll over and find Mona's side of the bed empty. I sit up in bed and can hear music coming from somewhere in the house. After taking care of business in the bathroom, I throw on a pair of pajama pants and head out to my family.

I find Mona at the stove flipping what looks like French toast while talking animatedly to both kids who are sitting at the kitchen island with plates in front of them. "Good morning." I ruffle Max's hair then kiss the top of Iris' head as I walk past them. I reach my woman and tip her head back so I can kiss her plump lips.

"Morning," she says against my lips. "Are you hungry?"

Does she know that such a simple question makes me want to eat her? Oh yeah, that twinkle in her eye means she knows exactly what she is asking. I whisper against her ear, "You are so bad."

"Here, let me fix you a plate. Go sit down, naughty." She pushes me away, and I take a seat next to Iris. Mona brings me a cup of coffee and a plate with a heaping pile of French toast on it.

I finish the last bite and groan as I push the plate away. "That was so good, honey." She starts cleaning up. "Nope, leave it. I've got clean up."

She and the kids go into the family room. After I start the dishwasher, I find the kids running out the French doors with Fluffy hot on their heels.

I drop down next to Mona and wrap my arm around her shoulders. "Breakfast was so good. Thank you."

Mona laces her fingers with mine. "You're welcome. Do you have anything planned for us today?"

I shake my head. "No, I just thought we could spend the day relaxing. Is that okay?"

"Of course. If you don't mind, I was thinking about sitting outside and meditating for a little bit."

It makes me happy that Mona is starting to be comfortable in my place. "You go do your meditating thing, and I'll keep the kids occupied."

Mona kisses me before disappearing down the hall. She returns a few minutes later with her little pillow, phone, and earbuds.

I follow her outside and call for the kids to bring the dog in and that we're going to let Mona have some peace and quiet. The kids take off upstairs, and I head into my office.

I'm watching some stocks that one of my clients bought when they were extremely low. If he sells them now, he'll make a killing.

A knock on the doorjamb has me looking up and finding my girl leaning against it, watching me with a smile on her face. I hold out my hand to her, and she comes into my office. I push back from my desk for her to climb on to my lap. "Did you have a good meditation?"

"I did. It's so beautiful out. Is there a park within walking distance? I thought I could take the kids for a bit if you have stuff you want to get done."

Yep, I'm completely in love with this woman. "There is, but give me ten minutes to shower and get dressed, and I'll come with."

I help her off my lap, and she walks to where the picture Iris made for me is hanging. I come up behind her and wrap her in my arms.

"I love you, Joaquin."

I press my lips to her temple. "That's good, baby, because I love you too."

EIGHTEEN

MONA

"How's the new book coming? I feel like I've barely seen you. I missed you." I flutter my eyelashes at him, and he laughs.

"You haven't been missing me. You've probably been having a good time with your boyfriend." He drags out boyfriend like he's a kid. "Seriously, how have things been going with you guys?"

My cheeks hurt from smiling wide. "They're really, really great. I love him, and he loves me."

Miles stands and pulls me into his arms. "That makes me so fucking happy for you and Iris. You both deserve it so much."

"Thank you. I'm seriously surprised I'm not dancing around singing love songs." My smile dies. "I am worried about Iris. She called Sam to invite him to Joaquin's on Halloween, and he told her that he'd be busy taking his son trick-or-treating. Do you believe that? He's the one who wanted to see her and get to know her."

"I'm sorry, but it's probably for the best. Let him ghost right out of her life. She'll be better off without him."

I sigh. "That may be, but she's met him and wants to know him. She wants to see her brother and sister. I hate that every time he calls or she talks to him she gets sad and disappointed, but I'm afraid if I don't let this play out then Sam will try to pull some shit."

"So you're just supposed to let this go on while my niece constantly has her heart broken? I'd like to kill that guy."

We're interrupted by Sierra and Victoria who pop into the office. "Sorry to just stop by, but I thought we could talk about the Halloween party and dinner when my *tio* Hector is in town."

"Sure, come on in. Victoria, this is my brother, Miles. Miles, this is Joaquin's cousin, best friend, and co-caregiver of Max, Victoria."

My brother walks toward her and takes her hand. He leans in kissing both of her cheeks. Sierra and I smile as we watch the little interaction. When he pulls back, the four of us stand in the middle of the office in complete silence until Sierra excuses herself and drags Miles out with her.

Victoria leans in. "Your brother is very handsome."

"He is. He's also an amazing man and is going to make a phenomenal father one day. I could give him your number." I smile when her face lights up.

"You'd do that?"

I hug the other woman who has become a friend. "Of course, and I'm serious when I say he's a good man. I mean, he stepped in when I got pregnant, and Iris' dad took off. He's done so much for us." I realize that I just spit all of that out, and she probably didn't need to hear it. "I'm sorry; I didn't mean to just blurt all of that out."

"Is he coming to the house for Halloween?"

I nod. "He is. Maybe you guys can talk." Her cheeks turn a deep shade of pink, and I lead her to the loveseat. "Now, let's talk about food."

I help Iris get her lavender and pink sparkly butterfly wings on before stepping back and admiring my work. She's wearing the wings, a unicorn horn, the tutu she wore for her end of summer party and pink leg warmers with butterflies all over them. I also put purple glitter eye shadow on her and pink lip gloss. Her blonde locks are in a fishtail braid with ribbon threaded through it.

At her class party, we had everything but the makeup. There just wasn't enough time to do it, and they didn't want the kids to have anything on during class that would distract each other.

My sisters and Victoria are dressed just like us, and Miles is coming dressed as a Jedi. Joaquin is wearing the Jedi Master t-shirt, but he looks damn sexy in it. Before I came in here, I helped Max get his costume on, and my mini-guy is the best looking stormtrooper I've ever seen.

"Are you ready to head downstairs?"

She nods excitedly. In the hall, we find Max who's acting like he's standing guard. "Halt, who goes there?" he says, his voice muffled by his mask.

Iris stops in front of him. "Duh … it's me, Max, your best friend in the whole wide world."

He leans in toward her. "I know. I'm pretending."

I stop in front of him. "Mona and Iris Collins are reporting for duty, sir." I salute Max first, and Iris copies me.

"Follow me please." He leads us downstairs to where Joaquin and Victoria are waiting. "I present to you Mona and Iris Collins, the unicorn butterflies."

We curtsy, then I go to my man, and he kisses me. "You look gorgeous." He turns to Iris. "You're the prettiest unicorn butterfly I've ever seen."

Iris smiles and wraps her arms around his waist. We take a few pictures before they take Fluffy out back to play. Victoria and I get all of the hors-d'oeuvres ready, and while we're plating them Greta, Heidi, and Miles show up—followed shortly by Nick and Sierra.

Nick is wearing a t-shirt that says FBI, female body inspector. I shake my head and smile. Joaquin wraps his arms around me from behind. "Can I get you something to drink?"

"Joaq, I never thought I'd see the day that you were pussy whipped, but you are." Nick's boisterous laugh has me laughing.

"Nick, you're lucky the kids are outside, or I might have to smack you." Of course, I'm teasing; I wouldn't.

"Beautiful, I know you could never smack me. I'm too good looking." He winks and grabs Sierra who stands next to him. Nick wraps her in his arms and kisses her. Their kiss goes from sweet to almost indecent.

Joaquin tells them to get a room, which I'm thinking isn't the best thing to say because they disappear.

He gives my sisters a quick tour of the house, avoiding the end of the hall where there's a spare bedroom and the door is shut, which it wasn't before. Downstairs we take various pictures of the kids and adults, and then Victoria takes one of Joaquin, the kids and me. It brings tears to my eyes because we look like a family; we look like we belong together.

Victoria and Miles stay back to hand out candy, and Nick, who rejoined us ten minutes ago, pulls a wagon that's full of drinks while we move through Joaquin's neighborhood trick-or-treating. We go from house to house, and I don't miss the looks my sisters and I get.

I swear I heard one of these bitches say that I must be the nanny and what they wouldn't give to have a night alone with my man.

The last time I hear someone say it I start walking in her direction, but Joaquin wraps an arm around my waist and hugs me to his side. "You're the only woman I see." He kisses my lips hard and then pulls back. "*Mi cielo,* I love you. You gorgeous butterfly unicorn."

I giggle like a school girl and wrap my arm around his bicep, and we follow behind our kids going to each door.

By the time we're back at the house, I'm

exhausted. We hit so many houses that the kids' bags were so full that they set them in the wagon. Of course, all of us adults can't resist the candy.

I'm sucking on a cherry Tootsie pop when Joaquin pulls it from my lips and pops it into his mouth. I try to get it from him, which ends with me on Joaquin's back while everyone laughs as I wrestle to grab it from his mouth.

Somehow I get around his back and latch onto his front. Luckily, the kids are checking out their haul inside and miss when I pull the sucker from his mouth, and our kiss turns heated.

My asshole sisters start catcalling, and our kiss ends. He places me on the ground and hugs me tight.

We walk Greta, Heidi, Nick and Sierra out not long after we get back and watch them drive down the driveway and out onto the street. When we step inside, we find Victoria and Miles sitting together at the kitchen island, drinking wine and talking extremely close.

I don't bother hiding my happiness about this. Joaquin grabs my hand and pulls me out of the kitchen, leaving them alone. "Is it wrong that I love the idea of them getting together?"

"No, and I like it too, but we need to stay out of it." He kisses me. "Let's go make sure the kids haven't eaten all of their candy."

Joaquin sits up with me still impaled on his cock. I moan softly as he sucks my nipple into his mouth.

My movements slow as I wrap my arms around his head, and he switches nipples, giving it the same treatment.

He grabs my hips and works me up and down. The sound of our flesh slapping fills the room. "Fuck, baby. You're so wet for me." Joaquin licks and bites up my neck until he reaches my ear. "Get on your hands and knees. I need to fuck you hard."

I climb off him and get on my hands and knees. My body trembles as I feel him get in between my legs. I feel the head of his cock at my opening before he thrusts inside. A cry leaves my lips as he bottoms out inside of me.

He glides in and out slowly until he picks up speed. I'll have bruises from Joaquin's fingers as he grips my hips tightly. He plows into me at a punishing pace.

"Help me get you there, *mi amor*."

I reach between my legs, rubbing my clit until I come. Joaquin wraps his arm around my chest and pulls me until we're both on our knees—my back is firmly against his chest. One hand is wrapped around my neck and the other is gripping my tit.

He thrusts up into me at a quick pace, prolonging the orgasm that rips through me. I feel Joaquin's teeth clamp onto my neck as he begins to come deep inside me. We hold our position as we pant, and my heart stops racing.

Joaquin's hand slides up to my chin. He turns my head and kisses me slowly. I whimper as he slips his softening cock from me. "I love you," he whispers against my lips.

Every time he says that I melt. I reach behind

me, wrapping my arm around the back of his neck, deepening the kiss before I pull away. "I love you too."

We both clean up and dress in our pajamas, then we check on the kids who are both passed out, so we climb into bed. Joaquin situates us until I'm on my side with him snug behind me. I fall asleep almost instantly.

I'm not sure what time it is when I hear Joaquin's bedroom door open. I hear small footsteps across the floor. My eyes fly open when I hear my daughter's sleepy voice.

"Joaq?"

Joaq shifts in the bed. "Iris? What is it, *preciosita?* Are you sick?"

"No." Iris sniffs. "You love me and Mommy, right?"

"Of course I do. I love you and your mommy very much." Joaq sits up in bed. "Sit next to me, sweetheart. What's got you upset?"

"Why doesn't my dad love me?" My heart breaks hearing the pain in my girl's voice.

I know I should say something, but there's a reason Iris woke Joaquin and not me. At this moment, I fucking hate Sam. I want to punch him in his big, stupid face.

"Oh, sweet girl. I don't think that's it. I just think sometimes moms or dads don't always do what they're supposed to. You know that no matter what you've got your mom, aunts, and uncle. You know what else?"

"What?" Iris whispers.

"You've got me, Max, and Victoria. Now, hop

on and I'll carry you upstairs and tuck you in." I hear rustling around and then my daughter's sweet giggles as Joaquin carries her piggyback out of the bedroom.

I sit up, waiting for him to return, and he smiles softly as he steps into his room. "Is she okay?"

"Yes, *mi amor*." He climbs into bed with me and pulls me into his arms. "I really hate that sonofabitch."

"I do too, but thank you for being so sweet to her."

Joaquin kisses my forehead. "It's pretty easy to be sweet to her. I meant what I said to her. I love that little girl so much."

We settle in bed, and he falls asleep pretty fast, but it's a long time before sleep claims me. I can't help the feeling of foreboding I have.

NINETEEN

JOAQUIN

My father's going to be here any minute, and I've been watching Mona flit around the kitchen, cooking all day. She's been wound tightly since yesterday. I told her that my father would like her, but then she told me that Sam's father basically called her a whore and said that she'd gotten pregnant on purpose.

She's worried that my father will feel the same way about her. To be honest, I don't know how my father is going to react to Mona and her lavender hair and tattoos. I could've told him ahead of time, but it's none of his business. I want him to like Mona because of who she is inside.

Yesterday she and Victoria went to the grocery store and bought all of the stuff they need to make dinner. They did a lot of the prep work last night with the kids. At six o'clock this morning I found Mona in the kitchen double checking everything.

"Baby, everything is going to be perfect. Stop

stressing." I place my hands on her shoulders and can feel how tight her muscles are. She tries to wiggle away from me, but I move my arms around her chest; I hold her tightly to me. "I need you to do something for me."

"What?" Her voice is tight. When I turn her around her face softens. "I'm sorry. I didn't mean to snap at you.

"It's okay. I don't want you stressing yourself out. Whatever you cook is going to be great. Now, I want you to go grab your pillow, phone, and earbuds and go meditate for as long as you need to."

I make her go sit in my office with the door closed so the kids will leave her alone. She ends up being in there for a half hour, and when she comes out she seems a lot more relaxed.

The front door opens and Mona looks at me with a deer in the headlights look. "It's all good, *mi cielo*." She wipes her hands on the black wide leg pants she's wearing. Her top is white with ruffles around the collar, short sleeves, and is fitted, molding to her body.

I grab Mona's hand as my father walks into the kitchen with his future ex-wife—she can't be older than twenty-five. Victoria joins us when she leads the kids in from outside. Max and Iris are both dressed casually; they're kids, and they don't need to be uncomfortable.

"Hello, Dad." I hold out my hand, shaking his.

He looks me over. "You're looking well, son." Dad looks down at Max. "Hello, Maxwell. Do you remember me?"

Max's full name is Maxwell, but no one but my

father calls him that. My son hates it, but tolerates when his grandpa calls him that.

"Hi, Grandpa." Max grabs Iris' hand. "This is my best friend, Iris."

Dad grabs Iris' hand. "It's lovely to meet you, Iris."

The sweet little blonde who owns my heart curtsies, causing everyone to laugh and breaking the tension. "It's nice to meet you."

"This must be Mona." He grabs her hand and brings it to his lips. "You're just as stunning as my son says." I roll my eyes when Dad kisses both of her cheeks.

"It's so nice to meet you, Mr. Pena."

"Please, call me Hector." He grabs his date's hand. "This is Chantelle. She's a fashion designer."

She kisses all of us on the cheek, and then Victoria leads them into our never used formal living room and grabs them drinks. The kids disappear into the family room.

While Mona prepares the hors-d'oeuvres, I grab us both a glass of wine. She carries the little tray with pumpernickel bread, cucumber, sauce, and topped with dill on it. I follow her into the living room. She holds the tray out to Dad and Chantelle—he takes one from her, but his lady friend declines.

Mona sits next to me and takes a sip of the wine I hand her. "Hector, how long are you in town for?"

"We're only here through Tuesday." A long weekend and then he's gone. Just the way I like it.

Dad and I talk shop while Victoria and Mona try engaging Chantelle in conversation. The kids come in to get appetizers with Fluffy bringing up the rear, and then they disappear again.

A timer goes off, and Mona excuses herself to go check on dinner. "You should've hired someone to cater this or we should've gone out," my dad announces.

"Mona wanted to cook for you. She's worked hard all day preparing dinner for us tonight."

Victoria excuses herself and goes to help Mona, leaving the three of us alone. "How is Maxwell doing with his studies? Ridgefield Prep is a wonderful school. He'll have so many doors open to him for going there."

"He's only in second grade. Max is learning how to tell time and basic sentence structure. It's not calculus."

Dad let's out a hearty laugh and takes a drink of his scotch. "Still a smart-ass." He looks at his lady friend. "My boy has a mouth on him. He's why my hair is gray." My dad is only fifty-five, but honestly, he looks like my older brother. I don't see any grays on his head. The man is vain, so I wouldn't be surprised if he colored his hair.

She smiles at my dad and then looks at me. "I bet you were a naughty boy."

What the hell? Of course, my dad just smiles at her.

Mona comes in. "It's time to eat." I get up and wrap my arm around Mona's waist. "I hope it tastes good," she whispers.

"Baby, it smells amazing." My girl made Beef Wellington for us and fried eggplant for her and Iris. I really don't like that she made something for us that she isn't going to eat.

We reach the dining room, and I'm in awe. She's got the good china out, candles lit, and the platters of food displayed beautifully. "You outdid yourself, baby." I love how pink her cheeks turn when she smiles up at me.

The kids sit on both sides of Mona, and she gets their plates filled so they can get started. Everyone digs in once they get their food, and conversation is light while we eat.

"Mona, what are you eating?" Chantelle asks.

"It's eggplant. Iris and I are vegetarians." Mona grabs her glass of wine and takes a drink. "She's never eaten meat, and I quit when she was a newborn."

My father rolls his eyes and looks at me with a raised brow. I shoot him a look I hope conveys that he better not say something. Thankfully, he doesn't.

After the kids finish eating, Victoria takes them to get cleaned up and then rejoins us. Victoria and my father talk about her mom. She's in Spain right now visiting family. All of us kids were born in America, and my father and Victoria's mom were born here as well.

Their older brother, my *tio Francisco*, was born in Madrid and actually lives in a beautiful villa in *La Moraleja*. My hope is to take Max there in the next year or two to see where we come from. Victoria and I always had an amazing time when we visited when we were younger.

"What do you do for a living, Mona?" Dad asks. "My son has been so tight-lipped about you. The only thing he told me was you were beautiful. I was thinking that he made you up.

Mona stiffens beside me, and I know immediately what's going through her head. I wrap my arm around her waist and pull her into my side. "I-I'm a tattoo artist. I run a tattoo studio with my three sisters."

"Are you educated? Did you have formal training?"

I give my father the *did you really just ask that* look.

"Actually, Hector, I graduated from Georgia State with my bachelor's in fine arts with a focus on drawing and painting. One of my paintings is still hanging in the gallery on campus." She drains the rest of her wine and stands, excusing herself.

As soon as she disappears, I turn back to my father and lay into him. "Did you seriously just ask her that?"

He holds up his hands. "*Mijo*, I meant no disrespect; it was just a question. Should I go speak to her?"

"No, I'll talk to her. You just be nice. I love her."

When my dad and Chantelle get up to take their leave, I lead them into the family room where we find Mona with the kids. She's sitting on the sectional with a kid on each side of her with their heads resting on her thighs, sleeping.

They exchange goodbyes that are stiff and awkward, and I walk them out. "We'll talk before Chantelle and I head back to Florida." I slap my dad on the back and lean in kissing her cheek.

Victoria steps up next to me. "I know he's your dad, but he's kind of a prick. I think your new mom is younger than Iris." She laughs.

"You're really fucking funny. Fuck, I hated seeing Mona shut down like that."

Victoria grabs my hand. "Me too. She'll be okay. She's made of tough stuff."

We head inside. Victoria disappears toward her room, and I head into the family room but find it empty. Upstairs, I peek in on Max and find him tucked in and asleep. I step into Iris' room, finding her passed out as well. I pull the covers up higher over her.

The other night she woke me up and asked why her dad didn't love her, and it broke my heart. I wanted to tell her that she'd be better off without that piece of shit. When I gave her a piggyback ride upstairs and put her on her bed, she looked at me with her big blue eyes and said, "I wish you were my daddy."

"I wish I was too." I stepped out of her room and shut the door.

Now I do the same and head downstairs to my room. I find Mona curled up on what's become her side of the bed, and I get pissed at my dad all over again. In the bathroom, I get ready for bed and then head into our bedroom.

Because yes, it is ours, and it's only a matter of time before I ask her and Iris to officially move in. I crawl into bed with my girl and pull her into my arms.

It's a long time before sleep claims me.

Mona left an hour ago to meet a client at the

studio. The kids and I are going to have a lazy day at home. Right now they're running around with Fluffy outside, but we got a stack of Blu-rays to watch and pizza to order.

I woke this morning to Mona's lips wrapped around my cock, sucking it until I came down her throat. She then crawled on top of me, hugging me tightly. That's when I knew that she was over what happened last night ... thank, God.

We snuggled for a bit and then got up and ready for our day. Unlike Mona's ex, Sam, I didn't give a fuck what my father thought. The man hasn't been faithful or very loving to any of his wives. I may respect him as a businessman and the fact he's my father, but as a husband or partner he's shit, and there is no respect there.

It's early and the kids are still sleeping so we're able to drink our coffee and snuggle on the sectional. A couple times I try to talk to her about dinner, but she kisses me or nuzzles my neck, obviously changing the subject.

The kids come down a little later and climb onto the couch, snuggling with us before Mona makes breakfast. My son and I are becoming spoiled by all of Mona's home cooking.

"Joaq?" Iris pulls me from my thoughts.

She sits next to me. "What is it, sweetheart?"

"Can you put my hair in a braid?"

This little girl has no clue she's got me wrapped around her finger because I'll basically do anything she asks when she looks at me with those baby blues. "Uhh ... sure, *preciosita*. Why don't you go get me a brush and hair tie, and I'll do my best."

She hops off the sectional and disappears upstairs to get those things. I pull out my phone and pull up videos on how to braid. Max stands in front of me. "What'cha doin', Dad?"

"Iris asked me to braid her hair."

My own son, the little traitor, starts laughing. "You don't know how to braid hair."

Iris comes racing into the family room. She thrusts the brush and rubber band into my hands. "Okay, sweetheart, where do you need to sit?"

She climbs on the coffee table with her back to me. I pull her closer so I can reach her. I watch the video one more time before running the brush through her blonde hair.

I separate it into three parts. "Max, come here." My son humors us and takes the section of hair that I hold out to him. It's slow going as I crisscross the sections of hair while Max holds the pieces that I hand him.

It's not the prettiest braid, but it's not bad for my first attempt. I grab my phone and snap a quick picture and then post it to social media, tagging Mona so she can see the braid.

I show Iris the picture, and she smiles. "Not bad, Joaq."

She climbs off the coffee table and gives me a hug. Max grabs her hand, and they disappear upstairs, probably to play video games.

Fluffy jumps up on the sectional and climbs onto my lap, spinning in circles until he finds his sweet spot, and begins his nap. My text alert goes off, and I see it's from Mona.

Mona: You're an amazing man, Joaquin

Pena.

I smile and then shoot her a response that I know will make her blush.

TWENTY

MONA

The weekend went by too quickly, and Iris and I were both cranky when we got up this morning. It's getting harder and harder to be away from my boys. I don't know if Joaquin is going to ask us to move in, and even though we haven't been together for very long, I think I'd say yes.

I still can't get over the fact that Saturday while I was at the studio he put Iris' hair in a braid for her; it wasn't the best braid, but it was a great first attempt. When I got home, or back to Joaquin's, I found the kids sitting on both ends of the sectional with their arms crossed.

My man stood and came toward me, kissing my lips. "They got into an argument about what they were going to watch. Iris called Max a butthole, and Max called her a booger face. I wasn't sure how you'd want to handle it, so I put them both in timeout."

I wrapped my arms around his waist. "You did the right thing with her. Thank you for handling it."

225

The kids made up and were best friends again not more than a half hour later.

As I pull into the parking lot of Sugar and Spice, heaviness fills my gut. It's hard pretending that I'm no longer affected by Hector's words, but I am.

The other night I was embarrassed when he questioned my educational background. Of course, it shouldn't matter whether I went to school or not, but just to assume that I was uneducated was judgmental.

In that man's eyes, I'll never be good enough for Joaquin. He'll turn out just like Sam's father, and it'll eventually cause strain between us. No, what we have is different than what I had with Sam. We've been together a short period of time, but I know our love is solid and real.

I let myself inside the studio and turn the lights on. I hook the Bluetooth on my phone up to the stereo system and turn on some *Led Zeppelin*. While "*When the Levee Breaks*" plays, I take my bag to the office and stick it in my desk drawer.

Today is my consult day. I meet with every client at least two weeks prior to getting their ink done. We discuss their design, size, and colors. Realism tattoos have always been my favorite to do. I love creating designs that look life-like. Usually, it takes at least two long sessions to finish them.

I print up the pictures of all of my consults and take them over to my desk. Along with the information that they submit online with the picture, I draw up a loose concept to start with. Then after meeting with them, we finalize plans.

I pull my hair up into a knot on my head and slip

226

on my glasses, getting to work.

Three hours later I've made some good progress. Greta and Heidi are here. Greta's confirming appointments for the week, and Heidi is getting her station ready for her first client.

My first consult walks in, and I take her back to my station where we get down to business. She wants a tattoo of her wedding bouquet on her back. We talk about the size of the tattoo she wants and the placement. I show her the initial drawing I did and take notes of the modifications she wants.

She's the best kind of client—she knows what she wants but will accept suggestions if something won't work.

Once we have it nailed down, we decide three appointments will be needed. I tend to take my time when I work on these pieces. "We may not need that third appointment, but it's better to have it booked just in case."

"Okay, great. I can't wait to get started." She pays her deposit and leaves. I throw all of the plans and the picture in a folder and take it to the office.

I turn to head out front but freeze. "What are you doing here, Sam?"

He's carrying a large envelope in his hands. My heart races when he shuts the door. "I need to talk to you." Sam scrubs a hand through his hair.

My eyes burn, and butterflies take flight in my belly. "Just say whatever it is you have to say."

He hands me the envelope and then backs away. "I-I've relinquished my parental rights of Iris. Child support is going to stop. If she wants to get to know Nixon or Nicole she'll have to wait until they're eighteen."

My mind is whirling right now. My ears begin ringing. I slap the envelope on the desk, grab my phone, and launch it across the room at him. It shatters when it hits the wall behind him.

"What the fuck, Mona!" He jumps to the side.

"You could've ignored us! You could've let us walk out of the ice cream parlor and never saw us again. You came here, asked to see her, and wanted to know her." I move toward him. "You sat right there"—I point at the loveseat—"and told me that you'd been thinking about her, that your wife was pissed that you had a child you weren't involved with."

Sam hangs his head. "I lied. She was pissed that I was giving you money and that I wanted to see Iris."

"What ... so she doesn't want you to see your daughter ... ever?"

He steps toward me and lowers his voice. "She's not my daughter—I feel nothing for her. I haven't been there for anything. She deserves a dad who is going to stop at nothing to always be there for her, to move mountains for her. That man's just not me."

Sam reaches out to touch me, but I back away. "I'm sorry, Mona, I really am."

I can't speak, I can't move as I watch the father of my child walk out the door and out of her life forever.

Sierra comes rushing in. "What did that asshole want? Are you okay?" She looks me over. "Honey, you're really pale."

"Can you cancel the rest of my consults? I'll call

them to reschedule." I grab the envelope and my purse and rush out to my car. I need to see Joaquin—he'll make me feel better about this. I reach into my purse to grab my phone, but I remember I smashed it into tiny pieces. "Shit." Hopefully, he's at his office.

When I reach the beautiful structure, I get lucky and find a spot half a block down. Inside I press the button for his floor. I've never been here before and can't wait to see where he does his stock brokering.

A very cute man sits behind a desk wearing a fitted suit. "May I help you?"

"I'm Mona Collins, and I came to see Joaquin. Is that okay?"

He smiles wide, and I get a glimpse at his pearly whites. "I've heard a lot about you, Ms. Collins. You're even better than he described. Go on back, surprise your man."

I step through the door and head into the back. This place is so fancy I feel like I shouldn't be here in my jeans and t-shirt. I find an empty desk outside the office I assume is Joaquin's, but voices from inside stop me from entering.

"*Mijo*, what are you doing?" Hector's voice is pretty recognizable.

"What do you mean?"

"What are you doing playing house with the tattoo artist? Women like her are good for a little fun, but not for marrying. Could you imagine showing up with her on your arm for a business dinner with her tattoos and purple hair? You'd lose clients immediately. What are teachers going to think if she shows up for parent/teacher conferences for Max?"

Tears run down my cheeks. I wait to hear
Joaquin defend me—to say something, but he
begins laughing. I can't listen anymore and hustle
out of there. As soon as the elevator doors open, I
sprint inside and exit the building.

I quickly run home, take care of the cat, and pack
an overnight bag for Iris and me. I need my girl, to
show her how much I love her and that we don't
need anyone. I grab my laptop so I can message my
sisters and Miles to let them know I'm okay.

I get to the school and lie and tell them there is a
family emergency and that Iris will return on
Wednesday. My girl comes skipping down the hall
toward me. "Mommy!" She throws herself into my
arms, and I have to blink rapidly to keep the tears at
bay.

"Hi, baby." I hug her quickly and say goodbye to
the secretary then lead Iris outside to my car. "Why
did you pick me up early?"

"Well, I decided that you and I need a day of
pampering. We're going to stay at a hotel and go get
our hair done and mani/pedis."

My girl lets out an excited whoop. We head
downtown, and I pull up in the valet of the Omni
Atlanta Hotel at CNN Center. The man takes the
keys as I grab our overnight bag and Iris' hand.

We get a room, and she excitedly presses the
button for the elevator. The doors slide open, and
we step on. We reach our floor and find our room,
and I let us in with our key card. It's gorgeous with
a huge king-size bed.

Iris squeals and runs into the room, diving for the

bed. My eyes sting, and acid burns my throat. How can someone not want this beautiful girl? How could someone throw her away like she's a piece of trash?

I drop our bags and run, jumping on the bed and landing next to her. We giggle ourselves silly as we snuggle on the bed and begin watching TV.

I should grab my laptop and email everyone, but right now I just want to hold my girl in my arms.

We watch a couple episodes of the Big Bang Theory before we head downstairs to go to dinner. We're walking down the street when I spot a hair salon up ahead. I lead Iris inside and stop at the reception desk.

"Hi, may I help you?" the pretty blonde asks.

I take a deep breath. "Umm, yes … I was wondering if you had any openings in the next couple of days. I'd love to get my hair colored back to its natural color. It's the same as hers." I signal to my daughter.

"Give me a moment, and I'll see if we can squeeze you in."

Iris and I look at the wall of hair care products while the woman does whatever it is she's doing.

"Ma'am?" I go back to the counter. "Today's your lucky day. We've had a cancellation. Can you come back at six?"

"Yes, that'd be great." I give her my name and let her know that we're staying at the Omni.

We head out to have dinner, and my stomach aches just thinking about getting rid of my lavender hair, but apparently my colored hair partly means that I'm a whore, will get pregnant on purpose, am

REALISM: SUGAR AND SPICE, INK

uneducated, and just not good wife material. Being a tattoo artist apparently solidifies that.

Iris chatters happily as we eat our veggie quesadillas, rice and beans, and chips and guac. When we finish, I pop a piece of gum in my mouth and give Iris one too. We head to the salon, and they get started on my hair.

Two and a half hours later, my hair is identical to Iris'. The girl did a great job and even did a deep conditioning treatment. It cost a lot, but I'm happy with the results. Of course, I can't remember the last time my hair was this color.

Back at the hotel, I pull out my laptop and connect to the Wi-Fi. I pull up the messenger app and send my sisters and brother a message.

Mona: I'm fine, Iris is fine, and we're just spending some time together. We'll be home sometime tomorrow.

Miles is the first to respond.

Miles: Where are you? Joaquin is freaking out. What papers did you leave at his office? Sweetheart, what happened with Sam? Please tell me where you are.

Mona: Iris and I just need to be alone right now. I don't want to talk about the papers. We'll talk tomorrow.

I close my laptop, and all I can wonder is why was Joaquin freaking out, and how did Miles know about the papers? I climb off the bed and look through my bag. Shit, where are they? I thought I shoved them into the bag, but maybe I left them at his office … shit.

JOAQUIN

"What are teachers going to think if she shows up for parent/teacher conferences for Max?"

I stare at my father for a beat and then laugh. "Are you serious? Mona has shown my son more love than his own mother ever has. She's got purple hair and tattoos, but she's got an even bigger heart."

I move toward my dad, who I've got four inches on. "Don't come into my business and insult the woman I love. The woman who is more than likely going to be my wife and the mother of any more children we decide to have. I don't give a fuck if she tattoos her entire face; I'll still love her.

"If I ever hear you say another word about her, you will be dead to me. I love you, you're my father, but you will not ever talk about her again. Do I make myself clear?"

I wish I had a camera to record the look on his face. No one ever stands up to this man, but Mona's ex never stood up for her, and I'll be damned if I'm going to let anyone ever insult her for being who she is.

"Okay, you're right, *mijo*. That was out of line. I'm sorry."

A knock on the doorjamb pulls my attention toward the open doorway. "Hey, Shane what do you need?"

"Mona Collins was just here, and she seemed upset when she left. She also dropped this." He hands me a large envelope.

"Thanks, Shane, I'll call Mona." I open the

envelope and pull the papers out. It's a copy of papers to relinquish parental rights signed by Sam. Jesus, she was coming here to probably show me those papers; instead, she overheard my asshole father.

I grab my cell phone and call Mona, but it goes right to voicemail. "Mona, baby, call me as soon as you get this."

I throw on my suit jacket, grab my wallet and keys, then stop in front of my father. "Have a safe flight home, and we'll talk soon." I slap his back and leave him standing in my office.

I head toward the studio because I'm sure that's where she's going.

TWENTY-ONE

MONA

"Did you have a fun time, sweetheart?" Iris and I are on our way home. This was exactly what we needed. I haven't been brave enough to tell her that Sam doesn't want to see her anymore; instead, we got our nails and toes done. In the fitness center we did their yoga class, and then we had a beautiful breakfast.

I drowned my girl in so much love, she'd see that we don't need a man in our lives, at least one not worthy of us.

I figure when the time is right maybe Miles can sit down with me, and we can talk to her about it together. We pull down our street and Iris cheers from the backseat. "Joaq and Uncle Miles are here." Their cars are both in front of my house.

Oh shit, I'm not ready to face him yet. I can't keep running. I just need to get closure and move on. I pull into the driveway, and Iris hops out. Joaquin and Miles step out of the front door, and my girl goes right to Joaquin who picks her up and hugs her tight.

"Mona, what the fuck?" Miles says quietly when he reaches me. "Look at your hair." He wraps his arms around me, hugging me tightly. "He's been worried sick about you. I'm going to take Iris with me for a bit so you guys can talk."

"I don't know if I want to hear what he has to say." I know I sound like a baby right now.

"You really should. I promise it's okay." He moves toward my daughter. "Come on, Iris. You and I have to run to the store."

Iris runs down the steps and wraps her arms around my brother. He lifts her and carries her over his shoulder toward his car. After getting in, they pull away from the house and disappear down the street.

I turn to find Joaquin walking toward me. I get a good look at him; he's got dark circles under his eyes, and his face is covered in dark stubble. He doesn't say anything; he grabs my hand and pulls me inside.

Joaquin sits me on the sofa, taking a seat next to me. I avoid looking at him, my eyes flitting around my living room.

"*Mi cielo? Mi amor,* please look at me." I finally looked up *mi cielo* a couple weeks ago and swooned when I read the meaning, but I can't think about that right now.

He grabs my hand in his much larger one and brings it to his lips. The moment my eyes find his, I get lost in those brown depths. "I know you were at the office. How much did you hear?"

A tear slips from my eye, and I bat it away not

wanting Joaquin to see it. "I heard from *Mijo*, what are you doing? Then I stayed through you laughing at the vile words your dad spewed."

His hands tighten on mine. "Baby, I was laughing because I couldn't believe what he was saying. I told him if he ever spoke about you like that again, he'd be dead to me." Joaquin lets go of my hands and grabs my face. "I would never *ever* hurt you like that. I know Sam made it so you're not trusting, but I love you. I'd love you if you were covered from head to toe in tattoos. I'd love you if you had piercings all over your body."

Tears roll down my cheeks, and I lean forward, pushing my forehead into Joaquin's neck. "S-Sam said he didn't w-want her. He s-said she wasn't his daughter and that he didn't feel anything for her."

My sobs are loud and ugly. I've been holding them in since yesterday, and it's killed me, but I couldn't let Iris see my hurt because that would hurt her more.

Through my tears, I tell him everything else that Sam said and how I threw my phone at him but missed.

"Sweetheart, I know it's hard and it hurts, but isn't it better for him to walk away now, before Iris gets any more attached to him? I know it doesn't feel like it, but he did the right thing." Joaquin hugs me. "Tell me why your hair is blonde." He presses his lips to my temple. "You and Iris look even more like twins."

"I don't know… I guess I thought about the stuff your dad said and the things that Sam's dad used to say and thought maybe I ought to change it up, then maybe people wouldn't treat me like I was an uneducated, man-trapping whore." I pull back from him.

Joaquin slides off the sofa and gets down in front of me. "I don't want to hear you talk like that again. You're an amazing woman, Mona, and I won't hear you say anything less." He grabs my hands. "You can't run away when stuff happens. We were all so worried about you."

"I-I'm sorry I made you worry." I wrap my arms around him and hug him tight. I slide off the sofa and land on my knees, straddling his lap. "I'm sorry that I thought you were laughing with your dad about the stuff he was saying."

"Can you do me one favor?" Joaquin kisses me softly on the lips.

I nod. "Yes, what?"

He grabs a strand of my hair. "I miss the lavender. Can you color it again?"

I smile. "Yeah, I can do that."

Joaquin kisses me as his cock moves slowly in and out of me. I moan against his lips as I feel myself getting closer and closer to orgasm. He reaches between us and rubs my clit until the tingling begins, and he gives me a firm thrust. My back arches beneath him as I come.

"Oh yeah, baby. You're squeezing me so fucking hard." He picks up the pace until he plants himself to the root and comes with a long groan. Joaquin kisses me behind my ear as he pulls out of me.

EVAN GRACE

He climbs out of bed and walks into the master bath, returning with a washcloth. He tenderly wipes between my legs and then tosses the washcloth into the basket. I throw on my nightgown and panties, and he throws on shorts, just in case.

Earlier when Miles and Iris returned, my brother stayed long enough for me to take him outside and tell him all about Sam's visit and the conversation I'm eventually going to have with Iris.

The more I talked about it, the better I felt. Sam was right, he's not her father. He may have helped create her, but that's it. My girl deserves a dad who's going to love her the way she deserves to be.

Miles even offered to be there when I finally talk to Iris about it, but I honestly think my girl will be just fine. She's a Collins girl, and we're made of tough stuff.

Joaquin pulls me from my thoughts when he drags me toward him until I'm draped partially over his body. "Thank you for staying here tonight. I just needed my girls under the same roof as me."

Why did I doubt him, and why did I run? This man has proven over and over again what a truly sweet, caring, bossy man he is.

"Of course. There's no other place I'd rather be." I fall asleep and do it smiling.

three months later

I carry the last of Iris' clothes upstairs to her room where Victoria and Heidi are helping me by putting my daughter's clothes either in the closet or in her dresser. "Here's the last of it. I didn't realize

239

how much stuff she had."

When Joaquin asked us to move in, I was afraid to say yes at first. I didn't want Victoria to feel like I was pushing her out, and I was afraid that Iris wouldn't want to change schools.

Victoria assured me she was ready to get her own place and knew that her boys were in good hands. She's actually going to be moving into my place once I get it all cleaned up for her. It's a nice, quiet neighborhood where the neighbors look out for each other, and since she's a single woman, it's perfect.

Well … I guess I wouldn't say she is single, but that's a story for another time.

Max was thrilled we were going to be moving in and had no doubts about it. Things have been going amazingly well these past three months. Our first Christmas together was beyond a dream come true.

I managed to get Joaquin and Max to wear matching pajamas with us Christmas Eve, and then our families came over Christmas morning for breakfast and presents. We all watched as the kids tore into their gifts, and when they disappeared to play with their new stuff, Joaquin handed me a jewelry box.

I carefully opened it and gasped when I saw what was inside. A pair of pink diamond studs sparkled at me. "They're beautiful," I whispered. I was overcome with joy and love and tackled him in front of everyone, not caring one bit.

I had no clue what to get the man who had everything, so I had a picture of the four of us blown up and professionally framed. Of course, I got him other little things, but I think he enjoyed watching the kids open their gifts most of all.

My brother, Nick, and Joaquin are taking my furniture that Victoria isn't keeping and putting it in storage. I was surprised by how much she wanted to keep, but most of the stuff I had I took really good care of, even with a child.

Joaquin wanted me to add touches of me to the house so I would feel like it was mine too. I honestly like how his home is decorated, but I did add pops of color with my crazy pillows and little knickknacks.

Pictures of Iris and me join pictures of the boys, decorating the walls now, and my clothes are hanging up in Joaquin's walk-in closet. When he gets back with the guys, he hands me a garage door opener since I already have the keys he made for me.

He leans down and kisses my lips. "Welcome home, baby."

EPILOGUE

JOAQUIN
one year later

Today I'm marrying the love of my life, and today I become Iris' father, even though she's been calling me Dad since the day I asked if I could ask her mom to marry me. I'm telling you, if that little girl ever finds out she's got me wrapped around her finger, it's all over. She'll be able to get away with anything.

The day before I proposed, I took Iris out for lunch. We made it a big affair, and it was hard to keep the reason from Mona. While we ate, I told her that I loved her and her mom and that if it was okay with her then I was going to ask her mom to marry me.

I knew she'd be happy, but I hadn't expected her to start crying. My first thought was she didn't want her mom and me together; instead, she got out of her chair and climbed onto my lap. Iris wrapped her arms around my neck and pressed her forehead into my neck just like her mom.

"Are you not happy, sweetheart?" I asked her softly.

She pulled back and looked up at me. "Does that mean you'll be my daddy now?" Iris sniffed and then wiped at her tears.

"If that's what you want, then it would be my honor to be your dad." She hugged me as she began to cry again.

"I love you, Daddy."

I'll never admit that I got teary-eyed when she called me that. We never did tell her about Sam signing his rights away because a month after he brought Mona the papers, Iris told us that she didn't want to see him anymore.

I've seen him out and about a few times, and I'd always have to take a deep breath, walking the other way to keep myself from punching that poor excuse for a man.

The kids went with Miles the night I proposed. It was a perfect night and she said yes without hesitation. Mona wanted to just go to the courthouse, but I put my foot down. This was going to be her one and only wedding, and I wanted to do it right.

We settled on getting married in our backyard, surrounded by family and close friends. I was happy to finally meet Mona's parents who thankfully were the complete opposite of mine. They'd brought gifts for both Iris and Max, welcoming my son into the fold with open arms.

My son had no problem calling them Grandma and Grandpa. Both of my parents showed up—they were civil, but they avoided each other as much as possible.

Nick comes walking toward me with a smile on his face. "Are you ready?

I nod. "I am. Have you seen her?" It's been hard not seeing Mona since last night, but she wanted to do this right.

Nick's smile gets bigger. "She's fucking glowing," he says as we walk toward the end of the aisle. Miles stands beside us—her brother got ordained so he could marry us.

Of course, my father wasn't thrilled we weren't having a Catholic wedding, but Mona's not Catholic, and I'm a non-practicing one. He's one to talk, though, because he's been married and divorced multiple times, which is a big no-no.

Sierra is the maid of honor and walks down the aisle and stops on the opposite side. Next up are Max and Iris, and I smile widely. My kids look amazing; Max is in black dress pants and a white dress shirt with no tie. Iris is in a white dress that hits right at the knees. The bodice goes straight across with thick straps over her shoulders. She looks like a princess.

The wedding march begins, and my girl appears at the end of the yard. She's wearing a dress that skims her curves. It's off-the-shoulder and her rose gold colored locks are in a twist on top of her head.

Her dad walks her toward me, and I don't miss it when she places her hand on her lower stomach, smiling so bright it's blinding. We've only told the kids that Mona is pregnant, and they're both so excited to get a baby brother or sister.

She's fourteen weeks already and feeling

fantastic. The plan was to start trying after the honeymoon, but apparently, fate had other plans. Mona's dad, John, reaches out and takes my hand.

"Take care of my baby," he tells me.

I nod and take Mona's hand, turning her until we face Miles. Everything else is a blur. When I hear kiss the bride, I grab her, dip her, and kiss the fuck out of her. Miles announces us as man and wife. Iris jumps into my arms, and Max hugs Mona around the waist.

Then I lead my family down the aisle, smiling the whole way.

six months later

I peek in on the kids and find that they're both passed out. I head downstairs, make sure the house is locked up, and then head into our bedroom. My wife is right where I left her, sitting up in bed with our two-week-old son, Daniel, latched onto her breast.

I climb onto the bed and move toward them, leaning down and kissing our son's head. I push myself up and kiss my wife on the lips. Mona rests her head on my shoulder. We've all settled into our new life pretty easily.

Iris is very much a mother hen and wants to do everything for her baby brother. We've had to set limits after waking up once in the middle of the night to find our son's bassinet empty. We panicked until we found him in his big sister's arms out in the family room. She claimed he was crying, and we weren't waking up.

Iris has backed off, but she does help her mom with the baby at night before bedtime. Max likes his baby brother, but he's a boy and not really interested in him. I know he was jealous that Iris was spending more time with the baby, but I promised him that once the newness of the baby wore off he'd have his best friend back.

Once Daniel is done nursing, I take him from my wife and place him on my shoulder. My boy burps immediately and then farts. I take him to the changing pad and quickly change him.

I place him in his bassinet and turn on the mobile above it. The soft lullaby has my son's eyes drifting shut in no time. I lean down, kissing his forehead, and then climb back into bed.

Mona immediately rolls into me, wrapping her arm around my waist. "He loves that song," she says quietly.

"He does, and pair that with being milk drunk, he's already asleep." I kiss her forehead. "Thank you for giving me so much I didn't think I ever wanted."

"Well thank you for proving that there are still good men out there, thank you for loving my daughter like your own, and just being a good man."

Her body gets heavy, and I know she's out. I hug her before rolling us until we're on our sides. As sleep claims me I feel a sense of peace wash over me and fall asleep smiling.

IRIS

sixteen years later

My mom straightens my train then comes around

to stand in front of me. "You look so beautiful." I blink to stop the tears from falling and smile at the woman who has given me everything.

"Thank you, Mom." I hug her and force the tears back.

The door bursts open and my sister, Celia, comes running in. Her pink bridesmaid's dress makes her look older than her fourteen years. I'm sure my dad threw a fit. He's a little overprotective of us girls, but Mom's just as bad with Daniel and Max.

"Wow, Iris, you're like a princess. Caleb is going to die when he sees you." She wraps her arms around me.

I hug my sister tight, and Mom quickly takes a picture of the two of us. A knock sounds at the door, and Max sticks his head in. When Caleb proposed, I knew no matter what that my brother, my best friend, was going to have to stand up for me. "Can I talk to Iris for a minute?"

Mom and Celia walk toward the door, both stopping to hug him before stepping out of the room. Max looks handsome in his tux. He looks so much like Dad that it's uncanny. His brown hair is styled, and his brown eyes sparkle as he smiles at me. "You look gorgeous, sis."

"I can't believe I'm getting married."

He stops right in front of me. "I should've never introduced you to Caleb." I know he's joking, but he *did* introduce us. Six months later we moved in together, and now we're getting married. "I just want you to be happy."

I smile up at him. "I am happy. Happier than I ever thought I could be."

Max pulls me into a hug. I'm thankful every day that we decided to kiss each other at the kiddie college when we were seven. That got us in trouble, and our parents were called in. The rest is, as they say, history.

Dad opens the door and comes walking toward me. "Wow." He stops next to us. "Max, give us a minute, would you?"

Max kisses me on the cheek before he disappears out of the room.

"Are you sure you're ready to get married? I can sneak you out right now." I know he's joking, and he really likes Caleb, but he was a little hard on him when we first started dating. He's had trouble accepting that I'm no longer a little girl.

"I'm sure, Dad." I wrap my arms around him. "I want to say thank you."

"For what, baby girl?"

I look up at him. "For everything. We may not share DNA, but you're my dad, and I love you so much."

He kisses the top of my head. "The day you called me dad for the first time was one of the happiest days of my life. I can't wait to see what the future holds for you. Let's say we get you married."

I loop my arm through his. "Let's get me married."

MONA

Joaquin pounds into me at a punishing pace. I cry out as my orgasm builds dangerously fast, but copious amounts of champagne seem to turn me into a wild, sexual creature.

My man thrusts once, twice, and a third time, planting himself to the root and coming inside of me. He kisses me before pulling out. After getting cleaned up, Joaquin climbs back into the bed and pulls me into his arms. "Our baby girl got married," I say quietly.

I did well with no tears until I watched my gorgeous husband walk our daughter down the aisle. Luckily, I had my brother and sisters close to give me support.

"She did. It was a beautiful ceremony, wasn't it?"

I nod. "It was."

Who would've thought that our kids getting in trouble would change all of our lives forever the way it has. I'll be forever grateful that our kids decided to kiss each other and that they got caught.

"I love you so much, Joaquin." I give him a squeeze.

He kisses my lips slowly and thoroughly. "I love you too, *mi amor*."

EVAN GRACE

SNEAK PEEK

Sugar and Spice Ink: Stencil
(Subject to change)
Coming: Summer 2019

I run to the bathroom just as the contents of my stomach come out. After I flush the toilet, I get up and brush my teeth. I crawl onto my bed and curl into a protective ball.

I can't shake this stomach bug. I've been sick for over a week now. Yes, I know one might think I was pregnant, but I took a test, and it was negative. Of course, it could've been too early or a false positive. Oh fuck, who am I kidding; I'm so pregnant.

I blow out a breath and grab my cell phone. I scroll through my contacts and find Dr. Honn, my OB/Gyn, and press the call button. When the receptionist answers, I give her my name and that I need to come in for an appointment.

I'm lucky, and they can see me on Thursday so I only have to wait two days. I don't remember my older sister Mona having morning sickness when she was pregnant with my niece.

I climb off the bed and stand in front of my full-length mirror. I grab the hem of my tank top and pull it up, turning to the side. My stomach is still flat for now, but do my boobs look bigger?

I cup them and give them a little squeeze. They don't feel bigger.

In the living room, I curl up on the sofa and turn on the TV. I watch Keeping Up with the Kardashians and can't help but wonder what I'm going to say to Nick. Well, I'm not saying anything until I get confirmation from the doctor.

More than likely he's going to run when I tell him I'm pregnant anyway. Our arrangement was just sex, wasn't it? It hasn't felt like just sex since our first weekend together.

I've tried to break things off multiple times, but either he ignores me or I come back because I can't get enough of him. It's like I've finally met my sexual equal. I always thought something was wrong with me because of my high sex drive, but I just love sex; better yet, I love sex with Nick.

Ugh, I feel like shit, and I'm still getting horny just thinking about him, but I'm not calling him until I know for sure what's going on.

"Well, Sierra, you're definitely pregnant." Dr. Honn smiles as she delivers the news. "You're due date is June sixteenth." She hands me a piece of paper. "This is a prescription for prenatal vitamins."

She goes over tips for the morning sickness and tells me she wants me to make an appointment for four weeks, and we'll try to hear the heartbeat then.

"Do you have any questions?" I shake my head because right now I can't think.

Dr. Honn walks me to the reception desk and congratulates me before disappearing in the back. Outside, I pull out my phone and dial Nick.

"Hey, sexy, what are you up to?" His voice alone makes me do a full body shiver.

I take a deep breath. "I need to see you. We have to talk."

Stay Tuned for more!

STAY CONNECTED WITH ME

Facebook Author Page
Facebook Reader Group
Goodreads Author Page
Twitter
Instagram
Amazon Author Page
Bookbub
Sign up for my newsletter and get the latest news

ACKNOWLEDGMENTS

First and foremost, thank you to my husband Jim. Whenever I'm on a deadline, you always step in, handling the cooking and cleaning while I work. I don't know how I'll ever be able to repay you, but I'm sure I'll think of something.

To my PA, Diane, thank you for all you do for me. You're my right hand, and I wouldn't be able to do what I do without you.

To Lydia from HEA Book Tours, thanks for always helping me spread the word for my stories and getting ARCs into the hands of readers.

Kaylee, thank you for always answering my many questions and for just being an amazing person and author.

My girl, Angela, thank you for always supporting me and for being a wonderful friend.

To my beta team Danielle, Jaime, Cassie and Teresa, this was a new thing for all of us, but thank you for your suggestions and catching stuff I missed.

Evan's Entourage, my most excellent readers group. I hope to have a lot more fun stuff planned this year and hope you're ready for an amazing year.

To Silla thank you for helping make my story the best it could be and for making it look pretty for my readers.

Ben my amazing cover designer, thank you for making me the most perfect and most beautiful cover ever. It was like you crawled in my head and knew exactly what I wanted.

AUTHOR BIO

A Midwesterner and self-proclaimed book nerd, Evan has been an avid reader most of her life, but one day an idea came into her head and a writing career was born. She's a sucker for happily ever afters and loves creating fictional worlds that others can get lost in. Evan loves putting her characters through the ringer, but loves when they get to that satisfying, swoony ending.

When the voices in her head give it a rest, she can always be found with her e-reader in her hand. Some of her favorites include, Aurora Rose Reynolds, (the queen) Kristen Ashley, Joanna Wylde, Madeline Sheehan and Harper Sloan. Evan finds a lot of her inspiration in music, movies, TV shows and life.

She's a wife to Jim and a mom to Ethan and (the real)Evan, , a friend and a writer. How does she do it? She'll never tell.

MORE TITLES FROM EVAN GRACE

RIPPLE EFFECT

A second chance romance

With Brock, I thought we had a love to last forever.

Until the night it died a quick, tragic death, leaving me broke, and destroying my ability to trust another man with my heart.

Now Brock is back and after years apart it's time to face my past and finally get some closure, no matter how much I still love him.

With Ripley, I was getting the home I had always dreamed of instead of the home I grew up in.

I grew up in a home filled with violence and hate. Unlike my father, I vowed never to hurt the people I love. Until the moment I did just that. Now, I'm out of the military, returning home.

I don't expect to see Ripley and haven't laid eyes on her since that night, but even after six years, the feeling I have for her are still there.

It's time for me to face the demons of my past--the same demons that Ripley's been fighting this whole time.

Can Ripley forgive me, and even if she does -- will I be able to forgive myself for hurting the only person

263

who ever mattered?

CHAPTER ONE

Brock

"Hey baby." MY girl, my heart, the love of my life climbs into my beat-up old Ford pickup truck. Once she's inside, I grab the back of her neck, pull her across the worn bench seat, and kiss her lips hard before pulling back. Her smile is like a beacon of light leading me to the promised land, and her cornflower blue eyes twinkle in the sunlight as she stares at me.

"Brock what is it? Is something wrong?" She worries her lower lip between her teeth.

I stroke her cheek with my fingertips. "No, nothing's wrong. I just love you." Pleasure fills me as I watch her lightly tanned cheeks turn an adorable shade of pink. Even after all this time, I can still embarrass her.

Ripley Brown and I have been together since our freshman year in high school—well, technically we did break up for a week the middle of our sophomore year, but that's it. We were each other's firsts, and if I have it my way, we'll be each other's lasts.

I pull into the parking lot of Aldridge High School where Ripley and I are seniors. In two days, we'll finally be out of this place, and then in just a couple months, she and I will be heading to Western Illinois University. My girl is going to be studying elementary

education and I'll be going to school for law enforcement.

We talked for a long time about our future and where we both wanted to go to school, and her parents have been great about it. They know we're serious about each other and her dad knows that after graduation, I plan on giving Ripley a promise ring. I worked my ass off this past year to be able to afford the ring I wanted to give her: a delicate gold band with her birthstone, a sapphire, and a little diamond next to each other. I really wantedto propose, but I know she wouldn't want to get married until we both finish college.

I can wait.

I climb out of my truck and walk around the front end, helping Ripley down then wrapping my arm around her shoulders. At our school, it's small enough that you almost know everyone. Sometimes it's a good thing, and other times not so much, like last year when a rumor was started I had cheated on Rip with some girl I met at an away game. It wasn't true; I'd never do that to her.

It all started because Jonah Mitchell is a rich asshole prick who thinks he's entitled to everything, including my girl. Ripley is the only girl at school who is immune to his "charm". Sure, she is nice to him—she's nice to everyone—but he is always watching
her, looking at her like he wants to strip her bare and do whatever he wants with her. We've hated each other since grade school, and I hate him still.

Once inside the building, we make our way toward our lockers, which are coincidentally right next to each other—thanks to Rip's best friend, Kat. Every year, the friends switch lockers, and it was actually Kat who introduced us.

Through grade school and junior high, Rip and I went to different schools. It was two days after the first day of high school that I met her and fell in love. I was putting my backpack in my locker when I heard laughter coming down the hall. When I turned toward the sound, I felt myself freeze. Ripley was walking arm in arm with Kat, and she was smiling widely at the spastic red head. My breath caught in my throat, and my dick took notice.

She hasn't changed much since then. Her blonde hair hung down her back framing her face in wild, crazy curls, and her eyes were the softest blue, surrounded by thick dark lashes. She was and still is a petite thing with subtle curves that do things to me, and it always brings out the need to protect her.

"Hey guys!" Speak of the devil. Kat races toward us, wrapping her arms around Ripley before letting her go and giving me a high five. "Only two more days then we're out of this bitch." She pumps her fist in the air, Ripley and I laugh.

"What's up, James?" I feel my body lock up tight and turn to find Jonah and the asshole brigade. They're your typical teen movie/teenage drama characters: rich boys who think they can do whatever they want. They hate me because I'm popular, captain
of the football team, dating the hottest girl in school, and what they would call poor.

My family is lower middle class, for sure. My mom works full-time, and my dad works until he gets fired then moves on to the next job because he's a drunk who loves to run his mouth. Everyone knows he beats us, or at least he used to beat me until I got bigger than him. Now he uses words instead of fists. He hits my mom, although she denies it and defends his shitty behavior.

I'll never understand why, and until she's ready to leave, there is nothing I can do.

I shake off those thoughts. "What do you want Mitchell?"

"Oh nothing." His eyes scan Ripley's body and I want to pummel his face, but that's exactly what the prick wants. He's been trying to get me to lose my temper for a long time, but I refuse to let that asshole win. "What's up Ripley? Looking gorgeous as always. You know if you ever want to come with me on my family's boat, I'd love to take you out."

I'm ready to pound him when I feel Ripley's arms wrap around my waist and her lips kissing the underside of my jaw. I smile, knowing what she's doing, and I attack her mouth right there in the hall, backing her up against my locker. She loves it when I pin her down or push her against the wall.

"When you're ready to stop slumming, I'll be here," Jonah says loudly, and I hear him growl before walking away. Reluctantly, I pull away from her.

Her grin is wide and she's got a hint of mischief in her eyes. "You're so bad. I'm going to have to paddle your ass tonight," I whisper against her lips.

Maybe I'll drive her out to our spot and make love to her in the bed of my truck. It sucks because I don't dare bring her back to my place, and her parents may love me, but they wouldn't if they caught us doing it in her bedroom.

"Promise?" Ripley winks at me before opening her locker and grabbing a pen, then gives me another kiss before disappearing down the hall with Kat.

I feel someone move next to me—it's my best friend Cale.

"What's up, dude?" We exchange one of those half-hug, halfback-slap greetings.

"Nothing." I look at my phone. "Running late?"

"Yeah, I couldn't get my fucking car to start. Luckily my dad was still home so he jumped it. Where are Kat and Rip?" Cale's got a thing for Kat, but is kind of shy around the opposite sex.

He's been really good about hiding his feelings for her, which is a good thing. If Ripley picked up on it, she would've already tried setting them up on a date. My girl is desperate to play matchmaker for everyone we know.

"They already took off toward Ms. Baker's class." I lean in close. "When are you going to talk to Kat? I don't want you to miss your shot with her before she goes away to school." Out of the four of us, she's going the farthest—she'll be attending USC and majoring in accounting. She's a freaky math whiz.

"I don't know. Every time I try to get her alone, it just doesn't work. Maybe I'll talk to her at Miller's party." One of our classmates is throwing a party the night of graduation. I honestly don't want to go because someone will get drunk and then get stupid, and it'll ruin it for everyone else.

Don't get me wrong, I like to drink, but I don't get all crazy with it because my dad's an alcoholic and I refuse to become one too. Plus, I wouldn't do anything that could jeopardize my relationship with Ripley.

"I think that's a great idea." I bump his shoulder. "Let's go before we're late."

My leg bounces as I wait for this graduation ceremony to get over with. We're finally graduating. I can't wait to finally be away from my dad. Of course, I don't want to move away from Mom, but she's never going to leave him. I wipe the sweat from my brow
and banish those thoughts from my mind. We've already been up to get our diplomas, and now we're listening to the final speech before we can get the hell out of here.

Ripley's parents are taking us out to eat after we're done and they invited my parents, but my dad said no, which meant my mom said no too. Whatever—I'd rather not have his drunken ass there. You know things are bad when every night you pray for your own father to drop dead. I've got a lot of anger inside me, and that's why I can't ever hit Jonah, even if I want to. I'm afraid I'll snap and there will be no turning back.

Kat taps me on the arm and I realize everyone is tossing their caps up into the air. I give her a smile and with a whoop, toss mine too. I spot Ripley as she comes running toward us, and I catch her in my arms. After spinning her around, I set her back down on her feet and kiss her quickly.

When I pull back, a flash has me turning my head—my mom is taking our picture.

"Let me take one more," she says with a smile.

Ripley wraps her arms around my waist and I wrap my arm around her shoulders. She snaps a couple more and then Ripley switches places with her. I wrap my arms around my mom, hugging her tight, and tell her, "I'm glad you came, Mom."

"I-I'm so proud of you. My baby boy is a high school graduate, and next, college." She kisses my cheek before taking her leave. I'm sure my dad told her when he wanted her home, and like always she does exactly what he says.

Ripley comes up and wraps her arms around my waist. "You okay?"

"Yeah, I am. Let's go find your parents."

CHAPTER TWO

Ripley

Brock moves slowly in and out of me, and my orgasm begins to fade. I can still feel him pulsing inside me after his, and my hands glide gently up and down his back. His lips touch that spot on my neck that makes goose bumps pop up all over my body, and a contented sigh leaves my lips. I whimper as Brock pulls his softening penis out of me. We both quickly dress, then

I lie back down in his arms. The bed of his truck isn't the most comfortable place to rest, but he keeps sleeping bags and blankets in a trunk in the back, which helps. "I can't wait until we go away to school," Brock whispers against my forehead.

I hug him tight and place my lips right over his heart. "I know baby. I wish my parents would let you move in until it's time to go." I push up and look down at him.

He reaches up tucking my hair behind my ear. "You know that's not a good idea. I love your mom and dad, and I'd hate if something happened that would change how they saw me."

Stuff like this is why my parents love Brock. He's always been respectful of their rules when it comes to me, and Dad has been instrumental in keeping Brock on the right path to graduate. His dad is useless, so mine took it upon himself to guide and support Brock's journey. That's why my dad's my hero.

Every day he drops me off at home sadness

washes over me as I think about what he's going home to. The first time Brock showed up with a black eye, I bawled like a baby and threatened to go after the bastard. Instead, my dad took Brock out back. I don't know what they talked about, but when they came back he grabbed my hand and we made our way to school.

I rest my head on Brock's chest. His heartbeat is a sweet, steady rhythm, and it's beginning to lull me to sleep. "How many kids should we have?" he asks quietly.

"Hmmm . . . well I'd like at least two, maybe three." We're both only children ourselves, but I have always wanted a big, loud, loving family.

He moves me so I'm on my back and he looms over me. "I think we should have four. I want a little girl that'll look like her mommy and three boys to protect their sister."

"Four? You realize I'm the one who has to carry them and then push them out, right? Although I do like the idea of having sweet little boys who love their momma." He bends down and our lips touch. The kiss is slow and sweet, and I could do it forever.

His tongue licks at my lips until they open to him, and the kiss quickly intensifies as our tongues tangle and my legs wrap around his hips. Then he pulls back.

"I need to get you home so you can get ready for the party unless you don't want to go anymore." He looks at me with a hopeful expression.

"We have to go. Come on, it'll be fun." With a sigh, he helps me stand up. We roll up the sleeping bags and blankets and put them back in the chest, and then he jumps down off the bed and reaches for me, helping me down.

On the way back into town, I sit right next to Brock with my head on his shoulder. All too soon, he's pulling up in front of my parents' house. "I'll be back at eight," he tells me before kissing my lips.

"Okay, I'll see you later. I love you." I climb out of the truck.

"I love you too, baby." I stand on the sidewalk and watch his truck disappear down the street, and then I head inside to begin getting ready for the party.

"Brock should be here any minute, so we'll just meet you there," I tell Kat as I pluck my outfit out of my dresser drawer.

"Okay, that sounds good. Cale offered to be my driver for the night and he just drove up, so I'll see you later." I toss my phone onto my bed and turn toward the mirror, wondering when

Kat's finally going to realize she and Cale could have something amazing, like Brock and me. I haven't said anything to Brock because he would accuse me of trying to mettle—which I am not doing—but if they need a gentle nudge, I'll give it to them.

The first time I met Brock, I thought he was a cocky jerk, but over our freshman year, I got to know him better. I never thought he'd be into a girl like me: shy and quiet, and my nose was always buried in a book. Kat was the outgoing one, the girl all the guys wanted. Heck, her locker was right next to his. The day he asked me out, that was all she wrote. After that, we were inseparable, and we still are.

My parents were a little worried at first because it was no secret the type of home Brock grew up in, and they didn't want me around Brock's dad. It didn't matter though, because he's never taken me there. Over the past three years I've only seen his mom
and dad a handful of times, usually in a public setting. His mom is a willowy woman who is beautiful, but constantly looks jumpy.

His dad is tall with brown hair that has some silver sprinkled through it, brown eyes, and a bit of a beer belly on an otherwise athletic frame. He would be a good-looking guy if I didn't know what a piece of crap he was. I hate knowing that his dad hurts him and his mom, and I don't understand why she stays. I've talked to my mom and dad about it, and they've never been able to explain it. The only thing they said was that if Brock's mom ever decided to leave, they would help her in any way they could.

I love my parents. My dad and Brock are close, and I love that he's taken Brock under his wing. He's a positive male role model for someone who's never had one. They've just made us promise to wait until after college before getting married and having kids.

I get back to the task at hand and quickly fishtail braid my ash-blonde hair so it falls over my shoulder in a thick plait. I touch up my eye shadow and blush then add a thin coat of pink lip gloss. . It's hot and humid so I throw on a black cami and a flowy lavender tank top that hangs off one shoulder. I slide on my favorite cutoffs, which are so worn, I'm surprised they haven't fallen apart. After slipping on my black Chucks, I head out into the living room.

My mom is sitting on the couch reading and I flop down right next to her. "Whatcha reading?" Since I can remember, my mom has always been a reader, always carrying a book around with her, which makes total sense because she's the head librarian at

Aldridge Public Library. I love to read, but not to the degree she does.

"Nora Roberts's latest book. You'd like it."

My mom knows what kind of books I like to read, so if she recommends it, I'm probably going to like it. "You'll have to let me read it when you're done."

"Is Brock picking you up?"

I look at my phone and see that he should've been here five minutes ago; he's never been late picking me up before. "He is, but he should've been here by now."

"I'm sure he'll be here any minute."

"Honey, stop pacing. I'm sure he'll be here soon." I turn to look at my dad while I dial Brock's cellphone again. It goes right to voicemail . . . again.

Something's wrong—I can feel it.

"Dad, what if he's in trouble? Can I borrow your car and go drive by his house?" Brock should've been here an hour ago. He hasn't called, and his is phone shut off.

My dad gets up and comes toward me. "Sweetheart, if he's not here in thirty minutes, then you and I will drive by." I frown, folding my arms over my chest. "You know why I can't let you go over there by yourself. I'm sorry honey, but I don't trust his dad. The answer is no."

At that moment, I hear Brock pull up, and I watch through the window as he stares at his steering wheel. Normally he'd be out of the truck and coming to get me, but he's just sitting there. My stomach turns as different thoughts go through my mind. I let the drape go, grab my purse, and head toward the door, only to be stopped by my dad. "Let me check on him first."

I can only nod as I watch him disappear outside and walk slowly out to Brock's truck. I head out onto the front porch. Dad leans against the driver's side door. They talk for a while and I'm getting worried, but then my dad steps back and Brock climbs out. That's when I see Brock's got a split lip and his cheek is slightly swollen.

With all of my might, I hold in the cry that is threatening to spill from my lips. My dad climbs the stairs first and I shove past him to get to Brock. He immediately wraps his arms around me. "Sorry I'm late."

I put my finger over his lips. "No, you don't have to apologize. Are you okay?"

277

He kisses my finger. "Yeah, I'm okay. You look beautiful."

I circle my arms around his waist and snuggle in under his chin. "Thank you. Let's go inside. We'll watch a movie."

"No, I'm good. I promised we'd go, so we're going." I try to argue but he shuts me up with a kiss. "This is our last high school party. We'll go hang out for a bit, then go see a movie, how about that?"

"Yeah, okay." I tell my parents bye through the screen door, mouthing a thank you to my dad.

We're both silent during our drive out to the Miller's farm. I want to ask what happened, but I'm afraid it could set him off, and I don't want to ruin our night. He lifts our intertwined fingers and kisses the back of my hand. "Two months."

I turn toward him. "Two months?" I'm not sure what he's talking about.

"Two months until we're moving to Macomb." A girly squeal escapes my lips and I squeeze an arm around his waist.

"I can't wait." We pull down the gravel road the farm is on then Brock parks his truck and I climb out the same side as him.

Hand in hand, we walk toward the huge bonfire. There are people everywhere.

"You're finally here!" Kat runs toward us and it's very clear that my bestie is hammered. I hug her as she sways, then she cups my cheek and Brock's. "I love you guys so much. You're going to get married and have beautiful babies, and live happily ever after." She pulls me in for a drunken kiss on the lips then kisses Brock on the cheek, and then just like that she's gone, off to do whatever she was doing before we got here.

Brock smiles down at me and I smile back, but my stomach knots up when I look at his split lip. I reach up and stroke it with my thumb. "Rip, it's okay. I promise." Nodding, I let him lead me over to Cale and other friends of Brock's from the football team.

I'm nursing my second beer when Kat drags me toward the makeshift dance floor. I smile at Brock as I sway to the music, and he gives me a chin lift along with a smile that makes my belly warm. One of his teammates grabs his attention so he signals to me that he'll be back then disappears into a mob of huge football players.

I'm finishing my second beer and dancing to the music with Kat and a couple other girls, but they've busted out the stripper moves. They're all shitfaced, of course. My best friend smiles at me before lifting her arms in the air and grinding on an invisible pole. I can only shake my head because that girl is so wild, but I'd do anything for her.

I need a drink, and before I go, I lean toward Kat. "I'll be right back. I'm going to get a drink and go to the bathroom."

"Do you want me to come with?" she asks.

I shake my head and wind my way through the thick crowd, stopping to talk to people and give out hugs. Brock and I haven't decided yet where we want to live once we finish school, so I may not see some of these people ever again.

By the time I make it to the porta-potties I have to go so badly. Luckily one is open, and I go in to do my business. Once I'm done, I check my face in the little mirror on the door, then I freeze when I step out of the stall. "Go away Jonah." Obviously my prayers that Jonah would skip the party weren't answered.

"Go away? Oh come on, don't be like that." I quickly move away from him, not listening to anything that jerk has to say. He doesn't even like me; it's just a game to him because he hates that Brock is better than him.

I know he's following me through the throng of people, but I refuse to look back and acknowledge him. I find Kat on the dance floor and keep close to her. I'm pretty sure Jonah is afraid of Kat because she's loud and in your face, and she has no problem telling people what she thinks. Last year at a house party, he kissed her and she slapped him across the face. My hope is dancing with her will keep him away, because I know he'll try to start a fight with Brock again if he can.

I begin to relax, figuring Jonah has slunk off to mess with someone else, and continue dancing. As I move to the beat, my eyes scan the different crowds as I look for Brock. I don't spot him, but I'm sure he's around somewhere. Arms wind around me and I smile because it's rare that Brock will dance with me. I place my hands on his and begin to move my hips, but then Kat freezes. She is looking at me strangely and I stop moving.

Brock's a lot taller than I am, and I suddenly realize the person against me isn't. I spin around and come face to face with Jonah then reach out and shove him hard with all my might. He grabs my wrists and pulls me toward him.

"Let me go."

"No, I don't want to. When are you going to stop slumming with that piece of shit? Baby, I can take you places you've never been. What can he give you that I can't?"

I'll blame it on the two beers causing me to lean forward and say, "Multiple orgasms." Of course, a crowd has gathered and they all whoop it up when I say it, but I ignore them and try to pull my hands free. Still, he won't let go.

The crowd parts and Brock comes over to us, followed by Kat and Cale. She must've gone and got Brock. I wrench my arms out of his hold and move to Brock. His arm immediately wraps around my shoulders and he hugs me tight.

"Mitchell, I thought I told you to stay the fuck away from Rip." Brock's body is strung tight, and I'm afraid he's going to freak out.

Jonah steps closer to him with a cocky grin on his face. Something ugly coils up in my belly and leaves me feeling uneasy. "It won't take long before she realizes she's hitched herself to fucking loser. How long do you think it'll take before she walks away from you? Apparently the only thing you can give her is orgasms."

A gasp leaves my lips as Brock advances on Jonah. I hustle to get in between them but Brock shoves me out of the way. I don't even think he knows it's me; his eyes are focused on Jonah. Kat grabs my arm to keep me from trying to stop them and says,

"Let Brock deal with it."

"I can't. Jonah's trying to push him to lose his temper and I can't let that happen." I move toward them and get between them both. "Brock, let's go. He's not worth it. Please." He still won't look at me and his body is held so tight, I'm afraid he's ready to strike.

"Brocky boy, how long is it going to take before you become your dad? Before you're nothing but a drunk and a wife beater?"

It feels like things move in slow motion. Brock tries to shove me out of his way and stalks toward Jonah. As I move right in between them again to stop Brock, I see his fist moving, hear screaming, and feel arms grab me right before I go down, and then…nothing.

Free with Kindle Unlimited

Amazon US
Amazon UK
Amazon CA
Amazon AU

Audible

BROKEN SOULS

She destroyed my family.

After ten years, Brylee Whitmore has returned to our home town, giving me my shot at revenge. I thought it would be simple, but she's changed. I was supposed to make her pay for what she's done, so why do I feel like I have to fix her instead?

Coming home was a mistake.

If my dad wasn't sick, I would have stayed away. Chase Foster plans to exact his revenge, and I deserve it. I'm supposed to pay for my sins, but now he wants to fix me instead. Too bad there's nothing left to fix.

One Tragedy.
Two broken people.
Can he forgive her?
Can she forgive herself?

CHAPTER ONE

Brylee

After disembarking from the plane, I make my way slowly down the tarmac. Everyone around me is rushing, probably rushing to family or friends waiting for them. No one's waiting for me, of that I'm sure. My mom did offer to pick me up, but my father is still recovering from the heart attack, and needs her more than I do.

I should've come sooner, but I just couldn't. Don't they realize how hard it is for me to come back to Barton? No, of course they don't because as far as they've been concerned, I should just get over it—I should move on, that it's time for me to start my life.

At baggage claim, while I wait for my suitcase I look up Uber on my phone and arrange for a ride. My thoughts start to drift to the past, but like always I try blocking them out. Great, just thinking about having those thoughts has me scratching at my wrists.

I drop my hands to my sides as the buzzer goes off signaling the arrival of our luggage. My gaze follows the bags as they move down the belt until it's on the track that goes round and round. I spot my suitcase and grab it off the belt. Toward the end on the line I spot my suitcase and grab it, pulling the handle out so I can drag it through the airport and out the sliding doors. I spot the red Camry and make my way toward it.

"Hi there, you're here for me." The man is old

enough to be my grandpa.

"Hello. Can I take your bag?" Taking my bag, his leathery skin brushes mine and I cringe. Contact isn't my thing, but as always, I push the thought down. Moving from the trunk he opens the front passenger side door. "You're welcome to sit up front…if you want."

"Thank you," I whisper and climb in.

The airport is twenty minutes from my home. I'm glad for the quiet as he maneuvers out of the parking lot. It gives me time to mentally prepare myself for my family reunion. Don't get me wrong—I love my parents and they love me, they're just different. They've just never been people who show a lot of emotion.

Cornfields fill my vision as we drive along the highway toward my hometown. The place where up until my sixteenth birthday had been my home. My haven is now a place I dread being—so much so that I haven't visited in a long time.

"Do you live in Barton?"

I turn to look at the driver. "No. I used to, but I moved to Chicago a while ago."

"What brings you back?" So much for silence.

"My dad had a heart attack." I tug my sleeve lower on my wrists. " I wanted to come home and make sure he's okay. They've already sent him home from the hospital, which makes me feel better." What is it with this guy that's making me talk? I've spent the last eight years keeping to myself and being invisible—just the way I've liked it, wanted it and needed it to be.

"It's amazing how quickly people can recover

and be home. I'm sure having you home will make the healing go that much quicker too."

I don't reply, just nod my head and gaze out the window.

Ten minutes pass and he pulls onto my street. Nausea settles in my belly and a lump forms in my throat. The grey ranch style home that I grew up in comes into view. As always there are beautiful flowers lining the walkway up to the house. The garden gnome that I painted for my dad when I was twelve still sits in the flower bed next to the steps.

My driver pulls into the driveway and shifts the car in park. My heart thunders in my chest.

I climb out and move toward the back. He hands me my suitcase. "I hope you have a good visit."

"Thank you." I mutter. Sweat drips down my spine and a shiver racks my body as I wheel my suitcase up the walkway to the front door.

I ring the doorbell and a minute later the door opens. "Brylee, you're here." My mom smiles and then steps back as I enter. Most parents would hug their children at this point, but instead, I get an arm squeeze. "How was your flight?"

"It was good. Luckily it's a short flight." My throat is scratchy. "Should I take my suitcase to my old room?" I'd rather stay at a hotel, but I should be here for my dad.

"Yes, I put clean sheets on the bed. Go get your stuff put away and then come visit with your father."

"Thanks, Mom." Turning to head down the hall, she stops me with a hand on my arm.

"We're so glad you're home. It's time to put the

past behind you." She reaches up and tucks a loose strand of hair behind my ear. "I knew it would take you some time, but that you would finally get over it, and come home for good."

They have always thought I should get over it. They will never understand why that day still haunts me. They don't get why I can't ever forget. Why I won't let myself forget. I've tried for years but it has never worked.

Numbness wraps around me like an old blanket and I welcome it. Anything to keep from breaking down. Answering Mom, I nod and turn down the hall to my room.

Opening the door images of my youth bombard me, I step inside and stand in front of my white wooden desk. Pictures of my friends and me cover the wall. On the desk I pick up my sophomore yearbook. I open it and the pages are smooth and cool to the touch as I flip through each page until I find the page with his photo, Chase Foster. Back then he wore his dishwater blond hair long. His ice blue eyes stare back at me with a familiar twinkle.

My fingers trace his full lips that are curled up in the corner in that familiar smirk he always wore. *Wait, what am I doing?* I slam the book shut and toss it in the trashcan.

Sitting down on the end of my bed I stare blindly at the photos of my past.

"Brylee come here." My best friend Kaylee *waves me over. The spunky blonde has been my best friend since kindergarten.*

I wrap my arms around her. "Hey!"

"Are you excited about Friday?" I nod. Friday I

turn sixteen and I'm pretty sure my parents are getting me a car. Then I'll be able to do whatever I want, within reason of course. My parents are on the strict side, but when I get a car, I can get a job and start making some money. Then I'll have more freedom.

"I'm totally excited. I'm just dying to know what kind of car they got me. You, me and Tiff can go driving around Saturday."

"It's so not fair that you're turning sixteen first." She glances behind me. "Chase is coming down the hall right now."

Chase Foster has been the star of my fantasies since I started having them. He's two years older than me and the most beautiful boy I've ever seen, but he doesn't even know I'm alive. All the girls want him and he's got a reputation of sleeping with anyone, but I've never been able to get his attention.

This past year I've learned how to wear makeup to highlight my favorite features and how to style my wavy chocolate brown hair. It's helped me get noticed more by boys at school, but they still don't want me like that. I know it's because of my body. I'm rather tall for a girl and also skinny with barely any boobs. I pretty much have the body of a young boy. I hate it but what can I do. I've tried everything.

I casually turn around to see where he's at. He's standing in front of the gym doors. His muscles on display give me a queasy feeling low in my belly. Chase is wearing basketball shorts and a T-shirt that molds to his muscled body. His hair is pulled back in the cutest ponytail.

288

I know I should look away before he catches me but I don't care. Something compels me to keep gazing at him. I hug my books to my chest as I watch him turn his head in my direction. My body freezes. Chase's eyes meet mine and he holds my stare. I know I'm blushing right now because my cheeks feel hot.

"Oh my God," Kaylee says behind me.

Chase walks toward me. He's got this lazy swagger that is so hot. He's almost to me when a couple of his friends stop him. Disappointment fills me, and just as I'm ready to turn around and head to my first class, he walks past me.

"See you around, Brylee." Then he winks at me.... He freaking winked at me.

Once he was out of sight, I look at Kaylee. "Did that just happen?" I whisper excitedly.

"He looked at you like he wanted to eat you up. Maybe he's going to ask you out." She starts clapping and jumping up and down.

"Maybe." We make our way down the hall to our English class and I can't help but smile. Things are starting to look up.

CHAPTER TWO

Chase

"Chase, your mom's on the phone." I look down at the back of the girl's head in my lap and sigh. She wasn't doing it for me anyway.

"Honey, get off my dick." My half hard cock slips from whatever-her-name's mouth and I stand up, tucking my flaccid cock back into my pants. The bleach blonde pouts as she stands up but I don't care. I don't look at her as I step around her and move toward the bar. If my mom can't reach me on my cell she usually calls the clubhouse.

I sit down at the end of the bar signaling Jared. "Need the bottle of Jack and the phone."

"You got it." Jared turns and moves down the bar. When he comes back he sets the black-labeled bottle in front of me and hands me the phone. I grab the bottle first and tip it back letting the whiskey slide down my throat, welcoming the burn. Taking a couple more deep swallows, I feel that familiar warmth that spreads through my body.

I tap a cigarette out of the pack after picking it up off the bar top. Placing it between my lips I quickly light it, blow out the smoke, and then pick up the phone, holding it to my ear. "Hey Mom, whataya need?"

"Chase Alan Foster, is that any way to talk to your mother?"

Scrubbing a hand over my hair, I sigh into the phone. "Sorry, Ma. What's up?"

I hear her sniffle into the phone and roll my eyes,

staring at the ceiling taking a drag of my cigarette. "Nothing, I just miss you. You haven't been by to see me lately."

"I know, I'm sorry. I promise I'll stop by this week. We'll order pizza." I take a drink of Jack. "Have you heard from Dad?" Eight years ago my dad up and walked out on us. I can't say that I don't blame him, even if he did leave twenty-year-old me to look after my mom. We all fell apart after Kyle died, but Dad took it the hardest.

Every now and then he shows back up, but only to get my mom's hopes up, only to disappear again, and again.

"No, not recently. I was hoping he'd be home for Kyle's birthday." Every year she makes me celebrate my brother's birthday. He'd be twenty-three this year. She'll make all of his favorite foods and a chocolate cake with vanilla frosting.

I know I shouldn't be encouraging this behavior but it gives her something to look forward to. "Maybe he'll show up."

My boss, mentor, and best friend, Loco, and yes that's his real name, waves me over. I don't like the look on his face; his brow is furrowed, and his mouth is pinched tight. "Ma, I've got to go. I'll call you tomorrow."

"Okay, honey. I love you so much. You know that right? Don't ever think that I don't. You and your brother have given me so much joy." She sniffles again and I close my eyes. I fucking hate this time of year.

"I know, Ma. I love you too. I'll talk to you tomorrow." I hang up and hand the phone to Ryan,

291

one of our newbies. I snuff out my cigarette, lighting another as I move through the bar toward the hallway that leads back to Loco's office.

"How's your ma?" Loco is full-blooded Apache Indian. He always wears his hair in a braid that hangs down past his shoulder blades. The man is pushing fifty but is built better than guys half his age. Hell, a couple of years ago he helped me get in shape after I got sober. *Fuck*, I had let myself go for a while there and it fucking showed. I'd had the beginnings of a beer belly, a puffy face, and constant blood shot eyes. Now, I still have my Jack, cigarettes and the occasional joint, but the hard drugs are done, and I'm in pretty good shape if I don't say so myself.

"Eh…Kyle's birthday is coming up so she's getting sad. Nothing that I can't handle. What's going on?"

He leads me into his office, and I don't have a good feeling when I notice that Grayson is sitting on the corner of the black lacquer desk. We've been friends since grade school and we've worked together since we were old enough to. I move further into the room and Loco stops right next to him. "What's up? You guys haven't come at me like this since I went on that binge."

Grayson crosses his arms over his chest. "Heard through the grapevine that a certain someone is back in town."

It takes a minute and then the brunette with eyes like mine flashes through my mind. The last time I saw her, her hair had been pulled back in a severe ponytail. She'd had pale skin, and was painfully thin with tears running down her face, but her face held no expression. It was like she'd been fucking dead, and I wish she would've been.

"So." I try to sound flippant.

"So?" Grayson sighs. "What are you going to do if you see her? You can't touch her."

I feel my lip twitch, wanting to snarl at Grayson. "Don't you think I fucking know that? I'd give anything to destroy that bitch, but I can't leave my ma. She just better hope I don't see her."

Loco moves to stand in front of me. I don't want to hear the words that are sure to come out of his mouth. "You have got to let that anger go. Your mom's forgiven her, why can't you?" He places his hands on my shoulders. "I know you hate her but that hate is going to eat you alive."

"She ruined everything. That fucking bitch destroyed my family." My ears are ringing—I'm so pissed.

Loco speaks slowly, quietly. "Chase it was an accident."

"I don't want to fucking hear it." I turn and stomp out of Loco's office, not stopping until I reach the bar. I spot the girl from earlier and motion her over with my head. The bleach blonde comes over, her hips swaying as she moves toward me.

"Hey Chase," she purrs as she wraps her arms around my waist.

I grab her and throw her over my shoulder, ignoring her squeals and carry her into the back. I let us into my room that I keep at the clubhouse, and it's really convenient for times like this. I throw her down on the bed. I watch her bounce up and down on the black comforter before I follow her down. Ripping her shirt up and off, watching her big, fake tits bounce I feel my dick start to get hard. In seconds I'll proceed to bury my dick in this random fucking pussy, and forget everything.

Free on Kindle Unlimited:

Amazon US
Amazon UK
Amazon CA
Amazon AU

Audible